Queen Milli of Galt

by Gary Kirkham

A SAMUEL FRENCH ACTING EDITION

FOUNDED 1830

SAMUELFRENCH.COM

ISBN   978-0-573-63339-3   Printed in U.S.A.   #14836

MUSIC USE NOTE

Licensees are solely responsible for obtaining formal written permission from copyright owners to use copyrighted music in the performance of this play and are strongly cautioned to do so. If no such permission is obtained by the licensee, then the licensee must use only original music that the licensee owns and controls. Licensees are solely responsible and liable for all music clearances and shall indemnify the copyright owners of the play and their licensing agent, Samuel French, Inc., against any costs, expenses, losses and liabilities arising from the use of music by licensees.

IMPORTANT BILLING AND CREDIT
REQUIREMENTS

All producers of *QUEEN MILLI OF GALT must* give credit to the Author of the Play in all programs distributed in connection with performances of the Play, and in all instances in which the title of the Play appears for the purposes of advertising, publicizing or otherwise exploiting the Play and/or a production. The name of the Author *must* appear on a separate line on which no other name appears, immediately following the title and *must* appear in size of type not less than fifty percent of the size of the title type.

PRODUCTION HISTORY

Queen Milli of Galt was first workshopped at Lamb's Players Theatre in San Diego, California.

The Premiere Production was at Theatre & Company Kitchener, Ontario. The Dramaturge was Henry Bakker with Set and Costume Design by Dennis Horn and Lighting design by Renee Brode. The Stage Manager was Nicole Lee and the production was directed by Stuart Scadron-Wattles with the following cast:

MILLI	Miriam Brown
EDWARD	Andrew Lakin
GODFREY	Alan Sapp
MRS. MILROY	Kathleen Sheehy
MONA	Alyson Scadron-Wattles

The second production was at the Chemainus Festival Theatre, Chemainus, B.C. The production had Original Music by Alexander Ferguson and Set Design by David Roberts, Costume Design by Robin Bowen, Lighting Design by Heidi Lingren. The Stage Manager was David Baughan. The production was directed by Jeremy Tow with the following cast:

MILLI	Katharine Venour
EDWARD	Mark DuMez
GODFREY	Bernard Cuffing
MRS. MILROY	Margaret Martin
MONA	Erin Ormond

HISTORY AND CHARACTERS

In 1972 Edward the VIII, living in exile, dies at the age of 78. Two weeks later, an eighty-year-old woman from a small town in Canada has her tombstone engraved, claiming to be his wife.

1972

OLD MILLI (82 yrs.): Millicent Milroy: a retired school teacher. Performed by the actor playing Milli.

JOURNALIST (20 yrs.): A young journalist. Performed by the actor playing Edward

1919

MILLI (29 yrs.): Millicent Milroy, a school teacher.

EDWARD (24 yrs.): Edward Prince of Wales, the heir to the throne.

MRS. MILROY (50 yrs.): Milli's mother, a widow.

MONA (30 yrs.): Desdemona Singleton, an actress.

GODFREY (50 yrs.): Sir Thomas Godfrey, Edward's handler.

QUEEN MILLI OF GALT is a work of fiction. Characters and locations are a product of the writer's imagination and are used fictitiously. Character names were only used for inspiration.

THE SET

The set is minimal, vague and dreamlike. There are three main areas: one that suggests a small house with a porch, another that suggests a garden, and one that suggests Edward's elaborate rail carriage. Branches with autumn leaves hang above.

Thanks to Henry Bakker, Stuart Scadron-Wattles and Jeremy Tow

Special thanks also to Chea Kirkham, Kerry Meads, Robert Smyth, Nick Cordileone, Cynthia Gerber, Linda Bush, Tom Stephenson, Ron Reed, Tom Vogel, Alan Janssen, Lisa O'Connell, Lea Daniel, Kate Holt, Robin Bennett, Darlene Spencer, Robin Schisler, Pat Northey and Olivia Olsen.

for Chea who made it possible

ACT 1

Prologue

(GALT 1972. Lights slowly fade up. A tombstone with the inscription:)

MILLICENT MILROY
1890-
wife of
EDWARD (VIII)
DUKE OF WINDSOR
1894-1972

(A single leaf falls and lands in front of tombstone. A young JOURNALIST enters, looks at tombstone, writes in his notebook, and picks up leaf. EXITS.)

Fade to black

9

QUEEN MILLI OF GALT

SCENE 1

(MILLI'S GARDEN 1972. The JOURNALIST is knocking at her door.)

JOURNALIST. Miss Milroy? *(Knocks.)* Hello, Miss Milroy, are you there? *(Pause.)* Miss Milroy? *(Sees MILLI.)* Miss Milroy I went up to the cemetery. I was wondering...

(OLD MILLI opens the main door, but keeps the screen door closed. She is just a silhouette behind the screen)

OLD MILLI. I told you, I'm not talking. Go, tell the others: "she's not talking".

JOURNALIST. The others have left.

OLD MILLI. And the television cameras?

JOURNALIST. They've all gone.

OLD MILLI. Why don't you leave too?

JOURNALIST. I want your story Miss Milroy.

OLD MILLI. You've got your story. A tombstone. A crazy old spinster. My goodness. What more do you want?

JOURNALIST. I was wondering...

OLD MILLI. Spinster... horrible word. I'm sorry, I can't talk to you.

JOURNALIST. Please... I need this interview.

OLD MILLI. I'm sure you do. I told the stone mason not to say anything... What did he say?

JOURNALIST. He said you were serious.

OLD MILLI. Well, there you go. I'm serious, I must be crazy. That's your story.

JOURNALIST. I want to hear your side.

OLD MILLI. Please leave me.

JOURNALIST. Could you... Just, just one quote. *(Pause.)* Just one quote.

OLD MILLI. Good day. *(She starts to close the door.)*

QUEEN MILLI OF GALT

JOURNALIST. No. No, please, wait, wait, wait! If I don't get this interview I'm out of a job.

OLD MILLI. *(Pause.)* They'd fire you?

JOURNALIST. Actually they fired me last week. *(Beat)* I get my job back if you talk to me.

OLD MILLI. *(Pause.)* I've just made some tea.

JOURNALIST. Thank you. Tha...

OLD MILLI. I'm not inviting you in.

JOURNALIST. Oh...

OLD MILLI. I've made tea: I don't want it to get cold. Good day.

(OLD MILLI closes door. The JOURNALIST sits down on porch, writes in his notebook for a while and then tears it up. OLD MILLI opens the door again.)

OLD MILLI. Are you still there?

JOURNALIST. *(Pause.)* Yes. I'm still here.

OLD MILLI. How long are you intending to wait out there?

JOURNALIST. I've all the time in the world.

OLD MILLI. But I do not. Good day.

JOURNALIST. Quite a pretty little garden.

OLD MILLI. I'm sorry?

JOURNALIST. Just admiring your garden.

OLD MILLI. Admire away.

JOURNALIST. What are those pink ones?

OLD MILLI. I'm not talking to you.

JOURNALIST. I understand.

OLD MILLI. I've better things to do with my time.

JOURNALIST. Quite a garden.

OLD MILLI. Not what it used to be.

JOURNALIST. Still quite something.

OLD MILLI. Cone flowers.

JOURNALIST. You'd think such pretty flowers would have a nicer name.

OLD MILLI. You think chatting about my garden is going to get me to talk?

JOURNALIST. Yes.

(OLD MILLI opens the screen door and comes out on the porch.)

OLD MILLI. Let me ask you a question. Do you believe what I put on the tombstone is true?

JOURNALIST. I'm here to find out.

OLD MILLI. That is not an answer. Yes or no, as it stands now.

JOURNALIST. *(Pause.)* As it stands now... no, Miss Milroy.

OLD MILLI. Honesty. You sure you're a journalist?

JOURNALIST. It would seem I'm not much of one.

OLD MILLI. *(Pause.)* I'll allow you one question.

JOURNALIST. Thank you.

OLD MILLI. But then you leave.

JOURNALIST. Yes.

OLD MILLI. *(Quietly.)* Then you leave.

JOURNALIST. Yes, yes. *(He reads his notes.)* Why did you put on your tombstone that you were Edward the Eighth's wife?

OLD MILLI. - Wrong question. Never ask why. *(Pause.)* You're not doing very well are you? *(Pause.)* I'll give you one more chance to ask the right question.

(JOURNALIST looks through his notes.)

OLD MILLI. I don't believe the question is going to be in your notes.

JOURNALIST. *(He studies OLD MILLI for a long while.)* When did you...? No. *(Pause.)* What made you think he...? Um... he hmmm. *(Pause.)* Humph... how...? *(Long Pause. He gives up.)* How are you feeling today?

QUEEN MILLI OF GALT

(Light change as the scene changes to autumn 1919. OLD MILLI transforms to the 29 year old MILLI dressed for gardening.)

MRS. MILROY. *(FROM 1919.)* Milli?
OLD MILLI. *(FROM 1972.)* I am feeling better today than I have in the last fifty years.

SCENE 2

(The scene gradually becomes...MILLI'S GARDEN Autumn 1919.)

MRS MILROY. Milli. Milli!
OLD MILLI/MILLI. Yes, Mother.
MRS MILROY. Milli! Are you going to change?
MILLI. I have changed.

(The young MILLI walks out into the garden. It is clear she feels at home here.)

MRS. MILROY. The lilac dress?
MILLI. No...
MRS. MILROY. The green dress?

(It is completely 1919. THE JOURNALIST is gone.)

MILLI. No. I'm wearing the blue one.
MRS. MILROY. Blue? Did you buy a new dress?
MILLI. No...

(MRS MILROY ENTERS.)

QUEEN MILLI OF GALT

MRS. MILROY. Then what dress...? You're wearing that old thing?
MILLI. I'm not going.

(MILLI is busy getting ready to garden and spends the rest of the scene getting her gardening tools, putting on her rubber boots and work gloves.)

MRS. MILROY. Well, of course, you're going.
MILLI. I've things to do.
MRS MILROY. Things? What could be more exciting than seeing the Prince of Wales?
MILLI. Almost anything.
MRS. MILROY. He's so handsome.
MILLI. There's a lot of gardening to do.
MR. MILROY. Everyone in town will be there.
MILLI. It's the first pleasant day in weeks.
MRS. MILROY. All the better to see the Prince...
MILLI. He's just a man... He puts his pants on one leg at a time.
MRS. MILROY. No, I think he has people to do it for him.

(MILLI takes an old brown sweater, holds it close to her face and smiles.)

MILLI. The Dahlias need to be dug up...
MRS. MILROY. Milli, I was going to make a whole day of it... Come with me. We'll do the gardening tomorrow.

(MILLI puts the sweater on.)

MILLI. I've school tomorrow. No. You go, enjoy yourself.
MRS. MILROY. You look so pretty in lilac.
MILLI. I'd rather garden.
MRS. MILROY. And miss the Prince?

MILLI. And miss the Prince.

MRS. MILROY. Mrs. Durham has seen him three times.

MILLI. She always comments on the purple Dahlias. We should give her some.

MRS. MILROY. She went all the way to Dundas to see him.

MILLI. All this excitement over a man.

MRS. MILROY. He's not just a "man".

MILLI. Stand all day, just to watch him walk by and maybe shake his hand?

MRS. MILROY. Do you think? Oh my... shake the Prince's hand?

MILLI. I thought the Prayer Circle wasn't going.

MRS. MILROY. We weren't. I mean, well, you know, he's worldly, smokes, and drinks. *(Beat.)* But... for the last month our prayer vigils have been... rapturous! Milli, I am going as a prayer warrior.

MILLI. Ahh.

MRS. MILROY. Milli, we feel God is going to do something wondrous. *(Pause.)* What do I do if he speaks to me?

MILLI. God?

MRS. MILROY. No, the Prince. What if Prince Edward, when he shakes my hand, speaks to me?

MILLI. Speak back to him.

MRS. MILROY. You're right! I could be the vessel the Lord chooses... But what if I say the wrong thing?

MILLI. There'll be thousands of people. I doubt...

MRS. MILROY. Or do the wrong thing? What if I curtsy wrong...? They do everything different over there... Mrs. Dowdy was giving lessons on royal etiquette. I don't think you're even allowed to look directly at him. Oh Milli, what if I don't know the answer?

MILLI. Tell him you don't know the answer.

MRS. MILROY. Oh I couldn't do that.

MILLI. Then lie to him.

MRS. MILROY. Millicent! *(Beat.)* I will trust God to give me the wisdom to say the right thing.

MILLI. Have you seen the trowel?

MRS. MILROY. God's wisdom.

MILLI. The trowel, Mother?

MRS. MILROY. I remember having it somewhere... Hmmm.

MILLI. I'll find it.

MRS. MILROY. But you're going to see Mona's performance tonight.

MILLI. I'll think about it.

MRS. MILROY. Desdemona Singleton! What was wrong with Mona Stankeiwicz?

MILLI. Nothing, Mother. Actresses never use their real names.

MRS. MILROY. The Prayer Circle wasn't too sure which name to use. Mrs. Powbottle said: "the Enemy would know her by Desdemona Singleton. And if we are to bind the Enemy and have her convicted of 'revelling in the sins of the flesh' we should use Singleton."

MILLI. Oh. She'd love to hear that.

MRS. MILROY. Well, if you're thinking about seeing Mona's performance, you might think about staying for the dance.

MILLI. I thought "dancing was a sin".

MRS. MILROY. No. It just leads to sin, dear.

MILLI. Oh.

MRS. MILROY. It's been so long since you danced. You'll catch the eye of many a young man.

MILLI. I have no desire to catch anything.

MRS. MILROY. Mr. Whiddelton's son, Jack, asked after you.

MILLI. "Whiddie"?

MRS. MILROY. There's also...

MILLI. ...No, Mother...

MRS. MILROY. ...Paul Macgregor, owns his own store, good Christian boy. Surely he's in your good books.

MILLI. If he were, I'd burn the "good book".

MRS. MILROY. It's been a year. It's been long enough, dear...

MILLI. Long enough?

QUEEN MILLI OF GALT

MRS. MILROY. There's no reason... You don't have to feel gui...

MILLI. Why would I feel guilty?

MRS. MILROY. You shouldn't. We've been sad... sad long enough. He would've wanted-

MILLI. Don't tell me what he would have... *(Pause.)* This is not about him. *(Pause.)* There's gardening to do.

MRS. MILROY. Yes... there is. *(Pause.)* Sorry, dear.

MILLI. Me too. I'm thinking of moving some of the foxgloves to the front.

MRS. MILROY. They'll look nice there.

MILLI. We'll give the hydrangeas one more chance, Hmmm?

MRS. MILROY. I don't want you to be sad, dear.

MILLIE. I'm not sad, Mother.

MRS. MILROY. But you're not happy.

MILLI. I don't need to be happy.

MRS. MILROY. Everyone needs to be happy. You have to be happy. You must be happy! *(Pause.)* Sorry, dear... You're right, Milli you... you don't have to be happy. I just want... I just want you to be happy. *(Starts crying.)* Happy. I just want... *(Sniffle.)* happy... a little... *(Sniffle.)* just a... little happy. *(Pause.)* Would it make you feel better if I... *(Sniffle.)* If I gave you a hug?

MILLI. I am fine.

MRS. MILROY. Really?

MILLI. I'm... *(Pause.)*I'll be fine.

(Long pause. MRS. MILROY is still weeping.)

MILLI. Would you feel better if I gave you a hug? *(MRS. MILROY nods yes. They embrace.)*

MILLI. You feeling better?

MRS. MILROY. Yes, dear, thank you, but, I wanted to cheer you up. *(Pause.)* I didn't even do that did I?

MILLI. Yes you did.

MRS. MILROY. Ahhh. So you're coming?

SCENE 3

(EDWARD'S RAIL CARRIAGE. At the Galt Station. There is the chatter of a large crowd outside and sound of the engine letting off steam. EDWARD and GODFREY are frantically searching for something.)

EDWARD. Where is it?!

GODFREY. Looking.

EDWARD. It was in my... Oh! It was, it was, in my... Where is it?! Where is it Godfrey?! Godfrey!

GODFREY. Let's see if it is not on the floor.

(EDWARD gets on all fours and starts looking.)

GODFREY. Sir, what are you doing?

EDWARD. Looking for it.

GODFREY. Yes I know, Sir, but you're on the floor.

EDWARD. Yes. If it's on the floor, then I have to be on the floor!

GODFREY. Sir, Your Highness, Sir. Please, please. Get up, Sir. I shall call in the staff. If we all looked...

EDWARD. No! No one should know about this, just you and I.

GODFREY. We shall look for it later.

EDWARD. No! Now!

GODFREY. But there's a crowd...

EDWARD. I'm not going out there without it!

GODFREY. Sir, please, they're waiting...

EDWARD. They can wait longer.

GODFREY. But Sir, we...

QUEEN MILLI OF GALT

EDWARD. The sooner we find it, the sooner we can get on with it.

GODFREY. Fine, Sir. Please get up, Sir! Sir, you can think about where else it might be.

(They change positions.)

GODFREY. You said it was in your pocket, Sir?

EDWARD. It was there, right there! It's not there now!

GODFREY. Sir... Your pocket... Is it possible you have a hole in your pocket?

EDWARD. I don't get holes in my pockets.

GODFREY. Of course.

EDWARD. Where could it be?!

GODFREY. Well...

EDWARD. Think, think!

GODFREY. Where were you last, Sir?

EDWARD. I've been with you! So where was I last?!

GODFREY. Don't worry, things don't just disappear. It has to be somewhere, Sir.

EDWARD. Well. That narrows it down. We now know it's somewhere.

GODFREY. Just trying to be...

EDWARD. Keep looking.

(We hear a band start to play God Save the King.)

GODFREY. Sir, we need to go.

EDWARD. Not without it.

GODFREY. Sir, I'll continue looking...

EDWARD. What if it's been stolen?

GODFREY. Sir! Sir, I will find it!

EDWARD. It's a sign.

GODFREY. I'll find it

EDWARD. We'll never find it! It's lost! What am I going to do? How could I?! Pathetic... Stupid! Stupid!

GODFREY. We'll find it, Sir.

EDWARD. No we won't! It's lost! (BEAT) You! You are supposed to make sure nothing goes wrong!

GODFREY. Sorry, Sir!

EDWARD. If you did your bloody job this would have never happened!

GODFREY. Sir!

EDWARD. I have a good mind to...

GODFREY. SIR!!! *(He stands up.)* Your Highness... when do you remember having it last?

EDWARD. During the speech. I told you...

GODFREY. In your pocket.

EDWARD. Yes. How many bloody times....

GODFREY. Right. *(He EXITS.)* It was cold.

EDWARD. What difference does that make?

GODFREY. *(O.S.)* It was cold! You wore your overcoat!

EDWARD. My...?

(GODFREY enters holding a well-worn but shiny teaspoon.)

GODFREY. Right where you left it. *(Beat.)* Sir!

(EDWARD takes the spoon, holds it and puts it back in his pocket. GODFREY starts to brush himself. Stops. He attends to EDWARD.)

EDWARD. Stop it. Stop brushing me! I was rude-

GODFREY. That's quite all right, Sir. You needn't...

EDWARD. Shut up. I said I was rude. I should not have said what I said. It's this bloody tour... Sorry.

GODFREY. I'm sorry for... I'm sorry also, Sir.

EDWARD. This bloody tour.

GODFREY. Let us "don our camouflage".
EDWARD. Yes.
GODFREY. It's time to become the Prince of Wales.

(EDWARD becomes the Prince of Wales and EXITS. There is the roar of the crowd. GODFREY brushes his pants.)

SCENE 4

(MILLI'S GARDEN. Later that morning. MILLI is on her knees planting bulbs. MONA ENTERS dressed in some outrageous fashion of the day.)

MONA. "And upon this fair land I do place my heart. How I have longed for the sweet smells of home."
MILLI. "And the joyous sounds of the ones I love. And so I dare say and..."
MILLI AND MONA. "say in earnest... And with tears and sorrow, and crying long. I am home."
MILLI. "I am home..."
MONA. "I am home!"

(They hug laughing.)

MILLI. Mona!
MONA. Ah sweetie.
MILLI. I really missed you.
MONA. I missed you too.
MILLI. Ahhh... Look at you...
MONA. I know. Outrageous isn't it?

QUEEN MILLI OF GALT

MILLI You're going in public like that?

MONA. All day.

MILLI. People will talk.

MONA. I hope so. But look at you.

MILLI. I don't...

MONA. If you spent half the time on yourself as you do on this garden of yours,

MILLI. I'd be a vain woman.

MONA. You could do with a bit of vanity.

MILLI. I haven't the time. Shouldn't you be there to see Prince Edward?

MONA. Why stand in the crowd when I can have him all to myself. Milli, I've got three dances with the Prince! Two Waltzes. And a Rag!

MILLI. Oh my. I have a friend who is dancing with the "Most Handsome Man in the Empire".

MONA. You could be at least a little jealous.

MILLI. I heard he was short.

MONA. I heard his smile takes your breath away.

MILLI. Then avoid his gaze and remember to breathe.

MONA. I shouldn't want to breathe too much.

MILLI. No, you wouldn't want to give him the wrong impression.

MONA. Oh, yes I would. *(Pause.)*

(MILLI stands up and gets a bushel basket of tulip bulbs.)

MONA. The paper says he'll dedicate the cenotaph. *(Pause.)* They're expecting you to lay a wreath.

MILLI. I know. *(Beat.)* What are you going to perform for "His Royal Highness"?

MONA. The Woman of Destiny Lane. They wanted something "to make the eyes misty".

MILLI. Ah. What scene?

MONA. Your favourite.

MILLI. Ahhh. My soul searches for my heart's love. Yet in this fog clad morn... I hear nought but wheelhouse drone. I abide on this pier. One woman waiting. This pier... where women wait alone, leave alone, and die...

MONA. Ah Milli.

MILLI. ...alone." *(Pause.)* I'm fine. It's just a play. I *(Beat.)* I don't know... I thought he'd come back! I... I never got the chance to tell him I loved... him.

MONA. He knew.

MILLI. Did he?

MONA. He knew. You didn't need to say it.

MILLI. I wish I had.You should have seen Jonathan at the station. He looked so smart in his uniform. I think it was the first time he wore something that actually fit him. He was pretending to be brave. We were both pretending. *(Pause.)* I was going to tell him then, I thought if I told him, then... then he would know. *(Pause.)*

MONA. What?

MILLI. He would know I thought he was never coming back. I thought if I didn't tell him I loved him, he'd... *(Pause.)* he'd have to come back. I know it's silly.

MONA. No, it's not.

MILLI. No, it's vanity. Thinking a man would cross an entire ocean just to hear me say, "I love you".

MONA. Jonathan would have.

MILLI. He's still over there. As if he never existed.

MONA. It's not fair.

MILLI. Why couldn't they bring him back? All they could do was carve his name on a cenotaph! *(Pause.)* I wanted to know how he... I wanted to know what happened. They didn't want to tell me, but I... I insisted. *(Pause.)* I needed to know. Now... *(Pause.)* Now every time I close my eyes I just see Jonathan in a... in a ditch, slowly dying. Alone in the mud. That's all I have.

MONA. Milli... I... *(Pause.)*

MILLI. What is it?

(Pause.)

MONA. Close your eyes.
MILLI. I've given up praying.
MONA. I know... close your eyes.

(MILLI closes her eyes.)

MONA. *(Pause.)* Now picture him.

(MILLI opens her eyes.)

MONA. It will be alright.

(MILLI takes a while but finally closes her eyes.)

MONA. Good, now picture him. You're picturing him?

(MILLI nods yes.)

MONA. And where is he? *(Pause.)* In the mud?

(MILLI nods yes.)

MONA. Now keep picturing him. *(Pause.)* He's closing his eyes...
and he's... he's dreaming of being... somewhere else. A special place.
Now where is that place?
MILLI. *(Long Pause.)* Orr Lake.
MONA. Orr Lake.
MILLI. He loved it there.
MONA. Orr Lake?

QUEEN MILLI OF GALT

MILLI. I know, it's not pretty. But... Orr Lake... it was quiet. He'd fish in his banker's suit. I'd read a book. We'd have a picnic. I'd bring too much food. We'd end up feeding this pair of black swans. They were always there. *(Pause.)* Always. He named them Myrtle and Chester. He said "such beautiful birds should have ugly names". *(Pause.)* It was a good place.

MONA. That's his place. *(Pause.)* Orr Lake. With Myrtle and Chester. Now. Good... picture his place... the lake... the swans... *(Pause.)* You see it?

(MILLI nods yes.)

MONA. Now picture Jonathan. Bring him across the ocean to be in his place... his favourite place. Good. You see him?

(MILLI nods yes.)

MONA. Where is he Milli?
MILLI. *(Pause.)* In the mud. *(Opens her eyes.)*

(Slow fade to black.)

SCENE 5

(EDWARD'S RAIL CARRIAGE. A few minutes later EDWARD is massaging his hands. Godfrey is writing in his schedule book.)

EDWARD. You see the size of that crowd? How many hands you suppose I shook?
GODFREY. Well about four or five hundred.
EDWARD. Felt like two or three thousand.

GODFREY. Well, yes, between four hundred and... two or three thousand.

EDWARD. We should have someone to count.

GODFREY. Maybe Lord Hamilton.

EDWARD. Does this hand look bigger to you?

GODFREY. Which hand, Sir?

EDWARD. The right.

GODFREY. Yes.

EDWARD. It is bigger, isn't it? All that "pump handling".

GODFREY. You do not have to shake hands, Sir.

EDWARD. It's swollen.

GODFREY. We could have you wave from the motorcar, Sir.

EDWARD. Waving from a distance? No! That's the King's legacy...

GODFREY. ...or walk with your hands behind your back.

EDWARD. It's actually bruised. I know how factory workers feel. Doing one movement over and over again. Horrid.

GODFREY. Shaking hands is a lot harder work than it looks, Sir.

EDWARD. It is work! Beastly work. I'm just like a factory worker.

GODFREY. Yes.

EDWARD. Except for the affluence.

GODFREY. There is that.

EDWARD. Maybe, we should tour a factory, you think?

GODFREY. The tour of the mines received favourable press.

EDWARD. I like the working class. You know... I could tell them that I'm a brother, that I know exactly how they feel: their life a monotonous groove. *(Pause.)* Yes! A factory tour sounds splendid. Watch out Godfrey, I'm becoming a Bolshevik!

GODFREY. We'll be flying red flags from the motorcade in no time, Sir!

EDWARD. *(Pause.)* You're right.

GODFREY. Sorry Sir, I misspoke.

EDWARD. No, you're right, I'm being... I just want to change... I need to change *(Beat.)* things.

GODFREY. I know Sir. *(Pause.)* I don't mean to rush you, but, we have a schedule to maintain.

EDWARD. I thought we're finished for the day.

GODFREY. Not quite, Sir.

EDWARD. What?

GODFREY. We have a few more speeches to...

EDWARD. A few more?

GODFREY. Yes, Sir.

EDWARD. I thought today was the slow day.

GODFREY. Tomorrow is the slow day.

EDWARD. Then what was yesterday?

GODFREY. Medium.

EDWARD. Medium?!! Yesterday was medium? Why did I think today was the slow day? Why don't I know these things?

GODFREY. Sir, your full itinerary is written in the notebook I gave you.

EDWARD. You know I don't read that!

GODFREY. It might help, Sir. *(Pause.)* Your itinerary for Galt, Sir: five speeches, two parades, a dedication of a Cenotaph, three meetings with local dignitaries, and one... dinner ball, Sir.

EDWARD. What?!!! Even bloody factory workers have breaks. But not the Prince of Wales!

GODFREY. I could give...

EDWARD. What happened to the fishing trips, a stroll through the park?!

GODFREY. Sir. I could arrange for a five minute stroll between events...

EDWARD. To hell with these stunts! I'm the bloody PRINCE OF WALES! Does that count for nothing? Godfrey, cancel something.

GODFREY. I don't have the authority to...

EDWARD. I don't care!Cancel something!

GODFREY. Sir, I cannot change a schedule that has the King's endorsement.

QUEEN MILLI OF GALT

EDWARD. He is not here.
GODFREY. But the King has ears everywhere.
EDWARD. What's next?
GODFREY. Sir, *(I cannot...)*
EDWARD. On the schedule, what's next?
GODFREY. Dedicating the Cenotaph.
EDWARD. Cancel it.
GODFREY. Sir... you understand I cannot...
EDWARD. Cancel it.
GODFREY. If it were within my power...

(EDWARD grabs the schedule from GODFREY.)

EDWARD. Then I'll cancel it.
GODFREY. Sir, you cannot defy the King's-
EDWARD. I'll do as I please.
GODFREY. Sir, you would be wise to...
EDWARD. Damn the bloody King!

(EDWARD throws the schedule on the floor. GODFREY slowly picks it up.)

GODFREY. I understand the immense strain you are under.
EDWARD. Yes.
GODFREY. Sometimes, Sir, sometimes we need to look adversity in the face and decide who is the better man.
EDWARD. Right.
GODFREY. If we keep a tight schedule, time will open itself up to you.
EDWARD. Yes. I just need one minute to myself. I can take a minute?
GODFREY. Yes, of course. We have five minutes till our next engagement, so take two minutes, Sir.

(EDWARD EXITS.)

GODFREY. *(Pause.)* The speech you gave this morning was quite touching. *(Pause.)* Sir? Sir...?

(GODFREY goes to where EDWARD exited. EDWARD is gone.)

GODFREY. SIR!

SCENE 6

(MILLI'S GARDEN. One hour later. MILLI is alone carrying a basket of bulbs. We hear the faint sound of a pipe band playing the end of a hymn. In the distance a Bugler begins to play Last Post. She stops. Silence. She kneels down and starts to dig in the soil. We hear a rifle salute. Another. And another. MILLI continues to dig.)

SCENE 7

(MILLI'S GARDEN. A few moments later. MILLI takes a basket, shakes out some rootstock, and splits it in half with a trowel. EDWARD ENTERS. He strolls along the sidewalk. He watches MILLI for a while before speaking.)

EDWARD. Good afternoon.
MILLI. Afternoon.
EDWARD. Beautiful day is it not?
MILLI. Mmmm.

EDWARD. Crisp, not too cold.

MILLI. Just right.

EDWARD. Beautiful. A little late for gardening?

MILLI. No.

EDWARD. Oh.

MILLI. I'm splitting my perennials.

EDWARD. Ah yes, of course. I'm terribly fond of gardening myself. Well, fond of gardens.

MILLI. Yes?

EDWARD. Yes, fond of gardens. *(Pause.)* Quite fond.

MILLI. Your accent, you're British?

EDWARD. Yes, quite.

MILLI. Are you...

EDWARD. Yes.

MILLI. ...travelling with Prince Edward?

EDWARD. Ahh... yes. Yes, I am... part of the Prince's retinue.

MILLI. Really?

EDWARD. Quite a pretty little garden.

MILLI. It's mostly dead now.

EDWARD. You still have a fair bit of colour.

MILLI. Fall blooms. Nature's gift before winter.

EDWARD. She puts on a marvellous show, does she not?

MILLI. Yes, she does.

EDWARD. I'd often heard about autumn in Canada. I was terribly looking forward to it. I was not prepared for how beautiful she really is. What's that tree in the corner?

MILLI. Sugar maple.

EDWARD. Extraordinary! Such, such, vibrant colour. It looks like it's on fire.

MILLI. That's what one of my children said... "The world is on fire and God puts it out with a blanket of snow."

EDWARD. Hmmm. Children. How many do you have?

MILLI. Twenty-eight.

QUEEN MILLI OF GALT

EDWARD. *(Beat.)* You are a teacher! Ahhh! A teacher. *(Pause.)* And your students call you...?

(MILLI stands, removes her gardening gloves and offers her hand.)

MILLI. My students call me Miss Milroy, and you are?

EDWARD. Miss Milroy. My friends call me David.

MILLI. You're travelling with the Prince... you must be a Lord or Duke or something?

EDWARD. Or something.

MILLI. The whole town is there to meet him.

EDWARD. Almost all.

MILLI. Yes! Well... And you?

EDWARD. I've escaped.

MILLI. You'll be in trouble?

EDWARD. You've no idea. *(Pause.)* Had to get away. I assume you, like me, find all that pomp deadly boring?

MILLI. There are other things I would rather do.

EDWARD. Most of it is a load of rot.

MILLI. Yes?

EDWARD. You didn't miss anything, just a speech or two.

MILLI. Yes, I heard they were quite dreary.

EDWARD. *(Pause.)* Really? I thought the people liked them.

MILLI. I thought you said they were a load of rot.

EDWARD. I assumed I was the only one.

MILLI. Apparently not.

EDWARD. People are always telling Prince Edward how much they enjoy his speeches.

MILLI. Yes. Who's going to tell The Prince what they really feel?

EDWARD. Who, indeed.

MILLI. *(Pause.)* You say you like gardening?

EDWARD. Well, yes, I like gardening. The idea. The gardeners do all the work.

MILLI. Garden-ers?

EDWARD. Lord, Duke or something.

MILLI. Ahh.

EDWARD. Well.

MILLI. Are you close to him?

EDWARD. The gardener?

MILLI. The Prince.

EDWARD. I have the Prince's ear.

MILLI. So you can tell him what you really think?

EDWARD. Well no.

MILLI. No?

EDWARD. I can never say what I feel. *(Pause.)* It's not allowed.

MILLI. Ahh.

EDWARD. Not allowed... although maybe, hmmm... Yes, maybe if I find out what other people think. You know... What they really think. Then I could pass it along to him.

MILLI. *(Beat.)* Oh no... I think not.

EDWARD. No, no, no, please! This would be so terribly helpful.

MILLI. The Prince would not want to hear what I have to say.

EDWARD. On the contrary. I would *(Beat.)* imagine... He- Prince Edward- would want to hear what you would have to say, I imagine. Not just two days ago he said to me. "David" he said, *(In an affected pompous accent.)* "David, I'm just mad to know what those splendid Canucks think of me."

MILLI. I'm probably not the best "Canuck" to ask.

EDWARD. Let me be the judge of that.

MILLI. I do not think this is a good idea.

EDWARD. Miss Milroy, you would be doing him a favour.

MILLI. I don't know.

EDWARD. If not for the Prince, then do it for your country.

MILLI. For my country?

EDWARD. Well... well then do it for me. *(Pause.)* Please. *(Pause.)* Please.

MILLI. *(Pause.)* Well...!

(Black-out.)

SCENE 8

(EDWARD'S RAIL CARRIAGE. Immediately from the Blackout. EDWARD is speaking to GODFREY in the darkness.)

EDWARD. What a vile little woman! What a horrible little- "The Prince is a bore"? Who does she think she is?

GODFREY. Where were you, Sir?

EDWARD. "The last remnant of a crumbling nobility"? "Does nothing"! "Shaking hands and waving like an imbecile"?

(Fade up.)

GODFREY. The entire staff is out looking for you!

EDWARD. This, this, this woman, this, this... woman!

GODFREY. Terribly embarrassing, a luncheon where the guest of honour is absent.

EDWARD. "The Prince is pompous, ineffectual". She called me "an imbecile"!!!

GODFREY. You can't just...

EDWARD. She said the most dreadful things.

GODFREY. What are you talking about, Sir?

EDWARD. This woman... this...

GODFREY. A woman approached you and said dreadful things?

EDWARD. No, no, no I approached her.

GODFREY. Just now?

EDWARD. When I stole away. I was with this woman.

GODFREY. Sir, if you had kept to the schedule...

EDWARD. She said the most dreadful things about me.

GODFREY. And she said you were an imbecile and a bore?

EDWARD. No, she said The Prince is an imbecile and a bore.

GODFREY. The Prince?

EDWARD. Yes.

GODFREY. But you are the Prince.

EDWARD. She thought I was David.

GODFREY. But you are David.

EDWARD. I know who... *(Beat.)* She did not know who I was! This is not so damn complicated!

GODFREY. Yes, she didn't know who you were. But, but you... you know who you are.

EDWARD. Yes, of course! What, exactly, is so hard to understand?

GODFREY. I understand completely, Sir.

EDWARD. Fine.

GODFREY. *(Pause.)* Why did she call you all these things, Sir?

EDWARD. I asked her to.

GODFREY. W... *(Why did..?)* We have a speech to give. And with a little effort we can get back on schedule. *(Long pause.)* Sir?

EDWARD. Godfrey. *(Pause.)* If I asked you what you really thought of me, would you... would you tell me?

GODFREY. Yes, Sir.

EDWARD. Would you lie to me?

GODFREY. If you asked me to.

(Pause.)

EDWARD. I'm just going to change.

GODFREY. I'll wait, Sir.

QUEEN MILLI OF GALT

(EDWARD EXITS. GODFREY laughs quietly to himself.)

SCENE 9

(MONA'S DRESSING ROOM. That evening. MILLI is alone. There is music and applause in the background. Reads from a tattered copy of The Woman of Destiny Lane.)

MILLI. "Ahhh, my heart doth beat,
And in it the rhythm of my lover.
Can I tell it to stop?
Can I tell it to not beat thusly?
No, it beats in my waking and in my slumber
Even my breathing is a silent song to my lover."

(MILLI laughs. MONA ENTERS.)

MONA. So this is where you are hiding?
MILLI. You did very well, Mona.
MONA. Thank you. Guess what-

(MRS. MILROY ENTERS.)

MRS. MILROY. Oh Milli! Good you're here. *(Pause.)* He looked right at me! He, Milli! And then... and then I shook — His hand. And He smiled!
MONA. He has the most gorgeous smile, Milli.
MRS. MILROY. He smiled! He smiled all the time but when I shook His hand, He smiled just a little more.

MONA. He's a real charmer. Guess...

MRS. MILROY. He's so wonderful. So very handsome.

MONA. Guess what, Milli?

MRS. MILROY. You can tell he is kind! He is The Prince, yet he cares about the common person. *(To Mona.)* Are you going to tell her?

MONA. I was about to.

MRS. MILROY. Tell her, Mona. This is such a great story! Oh Milli, this is such a good - Tell her, Mona!

MONA. As I was performing the scene from, 'The Woman of Destiny Lane'...

MRS. MILROY. Dressed as a harlot.

MONA. Dressed as a courtesan, Mrs Milroy.

MRS. MILROY. Tell Milli about the Prince!

MONA. Yes, I performed the scene, which went over rather well... I think I really-

MRS. MILROY. The Prince!

MONA. Would you rather tell the story, Mrs. Milroy?

MRS. MILROY. Yes, thank you! So after the play thing, the Prince asked our Mona for a dance! The first dance! Which was his choice... She didn't even have to use her card!

MONA. He asked me about being an actress. How I remember all those lines, how I am able to cry on stage. We chatted!

MRS. MILROY. The Prince chatted with Mona!

MILLI. You remembered to breathe?

MONA. Make fun if you want. But I have at least three more dances with him! At least three.

MRS. MILROY. Something you can tell your grandchildren.

MILLI. Yes, Grandma used to be a floozy.

MONA. A floozy who danced with the Prince of Wales.

MRS. MILROY. He's even more handsome up close.

MILLI. And you didn't faint

MONA. I felt a swoon coming on, but I held fast.

QUEEN MILLI OF GALT

(A waltz plays faintly in the background.)

MRS. MILROY. Ooh! They've started up again. You might get your chance.

MONA. Milli, it was dead fun. He's a great dancer, and so charming. I'll give you one of my cards.

MRS. MILROY. I'm pretty sure it isn't a sin to go.

MILLI. I'm not dancing, Mother.

(There is a knock at the door.)

GODFREY. Hello? Hello... Ahhh Hello, Miss Singleton? I'm Sir Thomas Godfrey. I represent Prince Edward. You were telling His Royal Highness you know the latest jazz dances. He is a somewhat tired of waltzes.

MONA. Yes! I know a few new steps. I'll just...

GODFREY. Good. You'll teach him. I'll get him presently.

(GODFREY EXITS.)

MRS. MILROY. The Prince! How do I look?

MONA. I wonder what he wants.

MILLI. He wants to learn some jazz steps.

MONA. Oh dear Milli. That's what he said. Men never mean what they say. Where are you going?

MILLI. I'll let you see Prince Edward on your own...

MRS. MILROY. No. No, Milli stay! You always miss out on any fun. Just stay. We can stay, can't we, Mona?

MILLI. You have a wonderful evening.

MONA. Just do me a favour...

(GODFREY ENTERS again.)

GODFREY. This way, Sir.

(EDWARD ENTERS. MRS. MILROY stands and does a strange bow/curtsy thing with a hand flourish.)

MRS. MILROY. Your Royal Highness. I am most honoured to make your most glorious acquaintance... again.

EDWARD. Likewise Madam. Ah, Miss Singleton. Are you sure you want to teach me? I'm not imposing?

MONA. Of course not, Your Highness. And this is my friend...

MILLI. Hello David.

EDWARD. Ahhh.

MILLI. It is David, isn't it?

EDWARD. Miss Milroy...

MRS. MILROY. You've met?

EDWARD. Miss Milroy, I can, I can...

MILLI. I imagine you could.

EDWARD. Let me explain.

MILLI. No need.

EDWARD. Please?

MILLI. Lord, Duke or something.

EDWARD. You have every right to be cross with me.

MRS. MILROY. You've met?!

MILLI. I should leave. I'm sure you don't want to see me again.

GODFREY. This is she?

EDWARD. Yes.

MONA. She?

MRS. MILROY. You've met?!!!

GODFREY. Miss Milroy seems to enjoy insulting the Prince.

EDWARD. Miss Milroy did not insult me. We had a discussion... she said what she thought.

MILLI. You asked me what I thought.

MRS. MILROY. When did you meet the Prince?

EDWARD. I tricked Miss Milroy into saying things she would not have said if she knew who I was.

MILLI. Oh, "she" would have said them in any case.

EDWARD. With a lighter touch.

MILLI. Actually, I thought I was holding back.

MRS. MILROY. Milli, what are you doing? This is the Prince!

EDWARD. I deserve this, she has every right. Miss Milroy, for my part, I am sorry.

MILLI. I accept your apology.

GODFREY. Miss Milroy, the Prince has apologized. You must reciprocate.

EDWARD. Godfrey, please! Pay him no mind. Miss Milroy, take your time.

(All stare at MILLI for quite a while.)

MRS. MILROY. Milli?

EDWARD. You have no intention of apologizing, do you?

MILLI. I have nothing to apologize for.

GODFREY. Madam!

EDWARD. No, Miss Milroy's right. She can't apologize for being what God has made her. It is its own punishment.

MILLI. And today punishment came in the form of a Prince.

EDWARD. Then I was of service.

MONA. I think the band has started up again.

EDWARD. Miss Milroy. I readily admit that I pretended to be other than I am. Rather... I was who I was... or am. I mean... Who you saw was who I... am.

MILLI. And to think I missed one of your wonderful speeches.

EDWARD. Behind soft features lies a sharp tongue.

MILLI. Behind sharp looks a dull wit.

GODFREY. Madam! Please!

MRS. MILROY. Milli. He's the Prince of Wales.

EDWARD. Miss Milroy, I'm unsure why you hate me so.

MILLI. I don't know you well enough to hate you.

EDWARD. Miss Milroy I'm...

MILLI. Don't take it personally.

EDWARD. Why would I take being called an imbecile personally?

MILLI. I didn't call you an imbecile. I merely said any imbecile could do your job.

MRS. MILROY. I don't know where my daughter gets...

EDWARD. I'm curious; do you treat all men with such contempt?

MILLI. Just the contemptible ones.

EDWARD. Ahh. It's not me you dislike.

MILLI. No, it's you.

EDWARD. It's men. You loathe men!

MILLI. Don't mistake my feelings for temperament.

EDWARD. Each time you open your mouth you prove me right.

MILLI. And each time you open yours-

GODFREY. Madam! Please!

EDWARD. You know, I have it on good authority, that I'm a relatively pleasant chap.

MILLI. Ah... so the fault lies with me.

EDWARD. Where are all the other pleasant chaps? *(Pause.)* No one to escort you, hmmm? A pretty woman like you. Surely Galt has a few suitable men?

(MILLI is silent.)

EDWARD. Not even one? I know your type all too well. There must have been a bloke, hmmm? Where'd he go? I know what happened to him. He got tired of waiting around. My thought is: you've scared him off. Poor sod never had a chance. You just never...

MRS. MILROY. Will you SHUT UP!

(All stare at MRS. MILROY.)

QUEEN MILLI OF GALT

MRS. MILROY. ... Your Royal Highness, Sir.

EDWARD. Miss Milroy... I was merely... *(Realizing the situation.)* Oh dear. I'm truly sorry, I was just... I was... *(Pause.)* Who was he, Miss Milroy?

MILLI. *(To Mona.)* I should go.

EDWARD. Miss Milroy...?

(MILLI exits. MRS. MILROY follows her. Stops and looks at EDWARD.)

EDWARD. Mrs. Milroy I'm...

(MRS. MILROY turns her back on EDWARD and EXITS.)

EDWARD. *(Quietly.)* I'm an absolute rotter, Miss Milroy.

MONA. I should go too, Your Highness.

EDWARD. Yes, of course. *(Beat.)* Miss Singleton, wait. I was wondering... *(Pause.)* Sir Thomas, would you excuse us?

GODFREY. Your Highness. Miss.

(GODFREY EXITS.)

EDWARD. Ahh... *(Pause.)* Miss Singleton, the mood seems to have turned away from dance. I came to learn a few new steps... and seemed to make all the wrong ones.

MONA. I should leave.

EDWARD. If you feel... *(Beat.)* I'll quite understand. But, please...

MONA. Milli is my friend.

EDWARD. A slow waltz perhaps?

(EDWARD stands ready to waltz. MONA eventually takes his hand. They start a slow waltz.)

EDWARD. So... tell me, how long have you known Miss Milroy?

(MONA smiles.)

SCENE 10

(MILLI'S GARDEN. Later that night. MILLI is sitting on her bench.)

MILLI. Jonathan? It's me. *(Pause.)* I think of you every day. The moment your train left the station, my heart presumed to imagine a story *(Pause.)* I imagined you crossed the ocean and arrived home to a cold angry girl whom you warmed with a smile. And right there, you proposed to her. You stumbled over your words. It was clumsy and silly and perfect. You surprised her. You always could surprise her. *(Pause.)* She wanted a small wedding. She filled the church with every single flower from the garden. She breathed in and never wanted to breathe out. On Sunday mornings you'd wake early and pick wildflowers that would wilt before finding their way into a vase. You let out a boyish laugh as she kissed your fingers that tasted of lavender. You put your ear to her belly and listened for a tiny heartbeat. You insisted on making "his" first toy. You turned a broken ironing board into a fine-looking rocking horse. She helped you with its mane. She used the wool from your old brown sweater. It smelled like... you. *(Pause.)* And when the sun went down you bundled up on the back porch. You drew her in close and in a warm whisper you boasted to the stars that you must be the happiest couple on earth. She forgave you for being "the war hero"... for being a little full of yourself. She forgave you for... almost... dying. *(Pause.)*

(A single leaf gently falls and lands behind MILLI. She does not see it.)

MILLI. Please... Please come out of the mud.

SCENE 11

(EDWARD'S RAIL CARRIAGE. The next morning. GODFREY has a telegram in his hand. EDWARD is dressing.)

GODFREY. Sir...

EDWARD. Dear God... From the King?

GODFREY. Yes, Sir.

EDWARD. What does he have to say to me?

GODFREY. Nothing Sir. It is addressed to me.

EDWARD. Ah... But it pertains to me.

GODFREY. Afraid so.

EDWARD. What does the "Old Man" want?

GODFREY. The King wants you to maintain the schedule as planned.

EDWARD. We knew that was coming.

GODFREY. And also to stop using personal anecdotes in your speeches...

EDWARD. What?

GODFREY. The King feels your "Little Asides", Sir, diminish the crown and demystify...

EDWARD. Demystify?! He wants to remain aloof and yet...! You'd think being six thousand miles away from the King would be far enough! How far do I have to go?!

GODFREY. He has ears...

EDWARD. Ears! "Ears everywhere". Who? Who is it?

GODFREY. It would be unwise to speculate.

EDWARD. Don't give me that shite Godfrey! Who is it?

GODFREY. I'm not certain.

EDWARD. I know you know.

GODFREY. I am not cert-

EDWARD. You're the only one I trust!

GODFREY. *(Pause.)* I should be mindful of... what one would say around Lord Hamilton, Sir.

EDWARD. Claud? We went to Osborne together.

GODFREY. It's only speculation.

EDWARD. That little twit. Why would he do this?

GODFREY. I believe the position of Consular General is opening up in New York, Sir.

EDWARD. That backstabbing... *(Pause.)* What should I do?

GODFREY. Better the Devil you know.

EDWARD. But I can't let him...

GODFREY. He will only be replaced.

EDWARD. Yes... There are many grovelers in the wake of the King's firm stride. I don't know how you've managed to stay clear of his wrath.

GODFREY. I haven't, Sir.

EDWARD. Really? But he would have punished you. He always pun... *(Pause.)* Oh no.

GODFREY. No, Sir.

EDWARD. Oh no, He didn't...

GODFREY. No, Sir, it's not...

EDWARD. The King is punishing you with me?

GODFREY. No, Sir.

EDWARD. The King sees me as punishment?

GODFREY. I wouldn't use the word "punishment", Sir.

EDWARD. That bloody sod!

GODFREY. Sir.

EDWARD. Am I that terrible?

GODFREY. The people, Sir. Thousands of them have been standing hours in the cold, just to...

EDWARD. Am I punishment?

GODFREY. Sir... *(Pause.)* I was offered the Paris embassy. I declined. *(Beat.)* Today's schedule, Sir: Meetings with the mayor of Toronto and the Premier. Dinner in your honour at the Royal British Society.

EDWARD. That bastard...

GODFREY. You will... Sir, you will be escorting a woman, Sir.

EDWARD. What?

GODFREY. Sir, I've narrowed it down to three.

(GODFREY has three hand-written notes on thick pressed paper.)

GODFREY. We have Mrs. Sparks. "I've thought fondly of our visit to Balmoral. Unfortunately we are unable to reciprocate an invitation as a couple, as my husband is visiting one of..."

EDWARD. No.

GODFREY. Next is a Mrs. Munro... "My husband and I enjoyed your stay with us at our villa in Coselleti. As fate would have it, I fell ill and could not accompany my husband who left yesterday for South America. I am glad to announce I have since made a full and speedy recovery." She sends a...

EDWARD. No.

GODFREY. ... photo. And finally we have a Mrs...

EDWARD. No. None of them.

GODFREY. Sir?

EDWARD. None of them. Fetch my car.

GODFREY. Well, Sir. We have a busy day ahead of us.

EDWARD. No, we don't. Fetch the car.

GODFREY. Sir, we...

EDWARD. I'm cancelling it.

GODFREY. You cannot...

EDWARD. It's just meetings with politicians.

GODFREY. But Sir, look at what happened last time.

EDWARD. Right. I'm cancelling it.

GODFREY. You must have a very good reason before we can change the schedule.

EDWARD. Godfrey, I just...

GODFREY. I could have you thrown by a horse.

EDWARD. *(Pause.)* Thank you Godfrey.

GODFREY. Sir.

EDWARD. I'll be back for the ball tonight.

GODFREY. Just remember to be stiff.

EDWARD. What?

GODFREY. Stiff... from being thrown by the horse.

EDWARD. Right. Remember to be stiff.

GODFREY. I'll fetch the driver, Sir.

EDWARD. I'll drive myself.

GODFREY. Sir?

EDWARD. Yes, Godfrey.

GODFREY. *(Pause.)* Have a safe trip, Sir.

EDWARD. I shall.

(EDWARD EXITS.)

GODFREY. Remember, Sir! Canadians drive on the wrong side.

SCENE 12

(MILLI'S CLASSROOM. Later that day. She is talking to her unseen students.)

QUEEN MILLI OF GALT

MILLI. All right, children, open your history books to page 57. *(Pause.)* When we last read of Henry Hudson, he was about to leave on his fourth trip to the new world. He was trying to find the Northwest Passage to China. He believed that the Atlantic Ocean was separated from the Pacific Ocean only by a narrow isthmus. And what is that narrow isthmus called today? Canada. Correct. He left in...

(There is a knock at the door.)

EDWARD. Excuse me, Miss Milroy. I hope I'm not bothering you?

MILLI. I'm in the middle of... *(Pause.)* Children, please...

EDWARD. They seem to recognize me.

MILLI. Yes. Children, please! *(Pause.)* Children... this is... *(Pause.)* This is The Prince of Wales.

EDWARD. Good afternoon, children. Miss Milroy, I was wondering if I could have a word with you?

(EDWARD takes MILLI aside.)

MILLI. *(Whispering.)* What are you doing here?

EDWARD. *(Whispering.)* I was wondering if I might have a little chat with your students?

MILLI. Children, please, quiet! *(Whispering.)* Why?

EDWARD. *(Whispering.)* Miss Milroy, I think I owe you...

MILLI. *(Whispering.)* You owe me nothing.

EDWARD. *(Whispering.)* ...an apology.

MILLI. *(Whispering.)* Well, you owe me that.

EDWARD. *(Whispering.)* Sorry. And don't reciprocate.

MILLI. *(Whispering.)* Your Highness

EDWARD. *(Whispering.)* Just a quick chat. I promise to behave. They might enjoy it.

MILLI. *(Pause.)* Children, I have a treat for you. Prince Edward is going to try his hand at teaching.

QUEEN MILLI OF GALT

EDWARD. Why, thank you, Miss Milroy. You're a lucky class. If I'd a teacher like Miss Milroy, I would have been a much more attentive pupil. *(Pause.)* So, who came to see me in the parade? Ahhh, Miss Milroy, it looks like all of your students were there. Well, Miss Milroy, what do you suggest I teach?

MILLI. Well, Your Highness, as chance would have it, I was just teaching history.

(MILLI hands EDWARD her pointer.)

EDWARD. A subject in which I am well versed. Miss Milroy and I had a discussion in which she said the Monarchy should be relegated to history. *(Pause.)* So, I guess the subject is... me! Do you have any questions? Yes? *(Pause.)* Jolly good question. Well, just a typical day for a prince. I awoke, polished my crown, had breakfast, saved a distressed damsel... and... oh yes, and I slew a dragon! *(Laughs.)* No, I'm fibbing, *(Beat.)* I didn't have breakfast. *(Pause.)* Yes, you at the back. *(Pause.)* No, I can't say I do. But if I did... Hmmm... most folks carry photos of their... family with them, I, on the other hand, just carry loose change. *(Pulls out a coin.)* That's my father right there. See? Can't get away from him. Can you all see? That's my father, what do you think? A friendly looking chap? *(Pause.)* Mean? Well, yes, he's not smiling is he? The King's not much of a smiler. The weight of the Empire on his shoulders and all. So he does his utmost to keep his smiling to a minimum. Here, I'll give it a try. How's this? *(Pause.)* You shouldn't be laughing. No, this is my best stern look. It seems I don't have the makings of a great king. Yes? *(Pause.)* If I kissed you, I'd have to kiss all the girls. *(Reacts to all the girls squealing.)* That means no! *(Pause.)* Yes... I... Yes, as a matter of fact, I was in the war. Not in the thick of things.

(MILLI reacts to hearing the boy ask about his father.)

EDWARD. Probably not, there were so many of us, 'over there'.

QUEEN MILLI OF GALT

The chances of knowing... But I am sure you are proud of what he did, and are glad he is back home. *(Pause.)* Oh. I see. Sorry. *(Beat.)* What was his name, son? *(Pause.)* Private Stanley Evans? Why... yes I knew him, he was... quite a man. I was privileged to serve alongside such a... brave soldier. *(Pause.)* No, no, I was not there when his... *(Beat.)* truck fell on him. *(Beat.)* You should be proud of your father. *(Pause.)* Yes, well, maybe in heaven. *(Pause.)* Well... Well, I must say that... that you are some of the finest children I have had the pleasure of meeting. And Miss Milroy, thank you for the opportunity.

MILLI. Class, let's all thank Prince Edward for spending some time with us.

EDWARD. No, no, thank you. Class dismissed. *(Beat.)* Wait! Miss Milroy have I overstepped my bounds?

MILLI. Well, Your Highness, it's not quite time yet... but if they promise to be very quiet in the hall...

EDWARD. Well then? *(Pause.)* Good. Class dismissed.

(EDWARD and MILLI watch the students leave.)

EDWARD. Master Evans. *(Gives a salute.)* It was an honour meeting the son of a war hero.

MILLI. *(Pause.)* Well...

EDWARD. I absolutely enjoyed myself.

MILLI. They were quite taken with you.

EDWARD. At least someone was.

MILLI. I... Thank you for visiting my class.

EDWARD. I thought I owed you as much.

MILLI. It was a very kind thing you did... Losing a father...

EDWARD. Yes. *(Pause.)* We lost so many.

MILLI. Having the Prince call his father a hero.

EDWARD. It was a small kindness.

MILLI. A small kindness he will remember the rest of his life.

EDWARD. Well...

MILLI. You surprised me.

EDWARD. Have I persuaded you to like me?

MILLI. Like would be too strong a word.

EDWARD. But I'm terribly likeable.

MILLI. Your Highness, every woman in the country adores you, and only one does not! Rejoice in the rest.

EDWARD. But they don't know me.

MILLI. Maybe that's the secret.

EDWARD. Miss Milroy, I've something horrid to ask of you. I was wondering... Would you like to be my guest for dinner this evening in Toronto?

MILLI. Me?

EDWARD. Yes, dreadful thing to ask of you.

MILLI. Dinner?

EDWARD. Yes, the meal one eats in the evening.

MILLI. Why would you want to have dinner with a woman who hates you?

EDWARD. It is preferable to spending it with a woman who loves me... for I cannot reciprocate. Whereas with you, Miss Milroy, I could learn to hate you. You make me feel at home.

MILLI. Your Highness...

EDWARD. It's just dinner, Miss Milroy.

MILLI. I think it's best we just end things here.

EDWARD. End? We'd have to begin something to end something. We haven't begun something, have we?

MILLI. No.

EDWARD. Good.

MILLI. Why me?

EDWARD. There's truth in your venom.

MILLI. Ahh.

EDWARD. "Truth in your venom". I believe I just called you a snake. Foot in mouth. You're right; I should just stick to waving like an imbecile.

MILLI. I appreciate the invitation, but...

EDWARD. Look Miss Milroy, I've driven fifty... sixty miles just to see you- Actually I got lost twice, so, closer to eighty miles. Let's just say, I've made an effort. And when one makes an effort, I believe it should count for something. And when a fellow is attract... And, and, and when I say "attracted", I mean as a person, not as a woman per se... not that you're not... a um... ah wom...*(Beat.)* You know, I should have written this down first.

MILLI. Dinner?

EDWARD. Dinner.

MILLI. With you?

EDWARD. Just you and me... and two hundred guests.

(Blackout.)

QUEEN MILLI OF GALT

ACT II

SCENE 13

(THE SOCIETY BALL. Later that evening. The sound of talking and laughing and a string quartet playing chamber music. GODFREY is waiting, he looks at his watch. He looks around and waits. He gives the slightest of smiles to the unseen guests that pass by. He waits and waits and waits.)

VOICE. *(Off stage.)* Ladies and Gentlemen: His Royal Highness the Prince of Wales.

(There is the sound of exuberant applause. EDWARD and MILLI ENTER. The applause increases and goes on for quite a while.)

EDWARD. Welcome to my world. It only gets worse.

SCENE 14

(THE SOCIETY BALL. An hour later. Laughter and chamber music plays in the Background. MILLI stands alone. EDWARD joins her. They

53

stand, looking and smiling at unseen guests.)

EDWARD. Thought I'd never get free. Are we enjoying ourselves? *(Pause.)* Don't worry, we are not supposed to. It is a society ball, Miss Milroy. One would be hard matched to assemble a more sordid company of individuals.

MILLI. They look pleasant enough.

EDWARD. Oh yes. Society functions bring out the most divine looking people, but, shall we say... "Something smells rotten in the state of Denmark".

MILLI. There is no smell.

EDWARD. Hmmm?

MILLI. In Denmark.

EDWARD. Really?

MILLI. It's just rotten, there is no smell.

EDWARD. I've been saying "smells" for years. You sure?

MILLI. Positive. "Something is rotten in the state of Denmark."

EDWARD. No one ever corrected me.

MILLI. No one is allowed to say what they really think.

EDWARD. Present company excepted *(Pause.)* So, Miss Milroy, it's time to don our camouflage.

MILLI. Camouflage?

EDWARD. I'm no longer David, Miss Milroy. Here I am Prince Edward. Notice the languid grin and the somewhat vacant look? Now, to enjoy such a stuffy event, we must peruse the crowd. *(Pause.)* See that large man with the sideburns?

MILLI . In the green suit?

EDWARD. George Sebastian Lubberts. Owns a shipyard and a silk factory. His mother lives in a rundown shanty with barely enough to sustain herself. Over there, the tall fair-haired chap?

MILLI. By the pillar?

EDWARD. Yes. Phillip Cordon Emrich the Third. As the name suggests, born into money. Fancies himself quite the gambler. Has nothing left. This will likely be his first decent meal in weeks. And the couple that just walked by? The Overmyeres. She has had affairs with half a dozen men here, including myself. *(Pause.)* Smile.

MILLI. Everyone knows all this?

EDWARD. The Society Ball, Miss Milroy. We act as if we didn't know what we do know.

MILLI. People enjoy these things?

EDWARD. We live for it. It all comes with years of practice.

MILLI. Interesting, Your Highness.

EDWARD. I'd rather you not call me "Your Highness". In your mouth it sounds like a slur.

MILLI. What should I call you?

EDWARD. We started off with David.

MILLI. But your friends call you David. I wouldn't want to taint the name.

EDWARD. Oh, it's been tainted. *(Beat.)* My family calls me David. *(Pause.)* So?

MILLI. We'll see, *(Beat.)* Your Highness.

(EDWARD and MILLI smile wider and nod to an unseen greeter.)

EDWARD. You were right.

MILLI. Hmmm?

EDWARD. About me being ineffectual.

MILLI. No, I didn't mean...

EDWARD. No, you were right. I am ineffectual. We, the British Royals, have been ineffectual for the last two hundred years. It's what has kept us alive. It's what has saved us from the fate of my cousin the Czar. Poor Nicholas he had no idea about the world outside his walls.

MILLI. But you do.

EDWARD. No, no, I'm just as unaware as he. Except I know I don't know. I'm keenly aware of my ignorance. I'm a waving smiling Czar, and you, Miss Milroy, are my little Bolshevik.

(MILLI looks at the crowd.)

MILLI. They do seem to love you.

EDWARD. They love what they think I am. *(Pause.)* So back to the game. The couple by the centre-piece?

MILLI. The older couple?

EDWARD. No, the younger. The ones smiling and talking through their teeth.

MILLI. Oh dear!

EDWARD. Seems we are not the only ones playing this game. They are, no doubt, speculating on your pedigree. "Who is that young woman with the Prince?" I imagine they have us enjoying a torrid affair. "She's the Prince's Canadian tart." Smile, Miss Milroy.

MILLI. How could they think that?

EDWARD. I presume most of the guests are speculating likewise.

MILLI. I doubt it.

EDWARD. Why not? As you know, they all see me as the most handsome man in the empire! And they see you, Miss Milroy, as an extremely pretty woman.

MILLI. Humph!

EDWARD. What a strange little sound. Do you doubt your beauty?

MILLI. I doubt the intent.

EDWARD. Don't worry, I can barely stand you. But from a purely objective point of view, you are what the lads in the army called "a real looker". They had other words but... Yes, a real looker. Smile. Yes, you have pretty eyes, Miss Milroy. Your nose is... I don't know, it's got character, in a charming way. Your lips, are rather, no, terribly alluring. I imagine most chaps here would certainly want to kiss them. And from what I can tell through your clothes and a healthy imagination, your bosom- Smile.

MILLI. Are you trying to seduce me, Your Highness?

EDWARD. David! No.

MILLI. Yes, you were! That was a terribly flawed attempt at seduction.

EDWARD. If I wanted to seduce you, I would.

MILLI. *(Laughing.)* Oh David. *(Milli tries unsuccessfully to control her laugh.)*

EDWARD. You can stop laughing now. Miss Milroy? It wasn't that funny. We are supposed to smile, not laugh. A slight titter perhaps. *(Pause.)* I'll start using my imagination again.

MILLI. *(Controlling her laugh.)* I'm sorry, David. I just... Hmmm, next time I'll try to... titter.

EDWARD. I don't believe you're the tittering type.

MILLI. What type do you think I am?

EDWARD. If I remember the song correctly, there are four types. The song in question is coarse and vulgar and not fit for your ears. But... you would be the fourth type.

MILLI. "The girl who claims she never has, but looks as if she might"?

EDWARD. You know the song.

(GODFREY ENTERS and whispers in EDWARD'S ear.)

EDWARD. Duty calls... again *(He nods at guest.)* David must become the Prince of Wales. Godfrey, would you keep Miss Milroy company.

GODFREY. Sir.

EDWARD. Miss Milroy.

(As EDWARD EXITS GODFREY clears his throat. EDWARD looks back. GODFREY makes small gesture with head. EDWARD exits faking "stiffness". GODFREY and MILLI exchange polite smiles. Long awkward pause.)

GODFREY. Miss Milroy. May I get you a drink?

MILLI. I'm fine, Sir Thomas. *(Long Pause.)* Surprised to see me here?

GODFREY. Quite.

MILLI. You didn't think he would invite me?

GODFREY. I didn't think you would accept, Miss Milroy.

(Pause.)

GODFREY. Did you have a pleasant drive, Miss Milroy?

MILLI. Yes... we did.

GODFREY. Did "we" get lost?

MILLI. Twice.

GODFREY. His Royal Highness has not mastered the twined skills of talking and driving.

MILLI. It would seem not.

GODFREY. Count yourself as privileged.

MILLI. I was under the impression he has a lot of lady friends.

GODFREY. None I would call friends, Miss Milroy.

(They hear EDWARD laughing.)

MILLI. It looks like the Prince is enjoying himself.

GODFREY. Yes, it does look like that.

MILLI. Camouflage.

GODFREY. *(Pause.)* Yes.

MILLI. They're all watching him.

GODFREY. They're asking themselves: "Does he have the makings of a great king?"

MILLI. And does he?

GODFREY. I would not be here if I thought otherwise. *(Pause.)* They all want something from him. *(Beat.)* Everyone, Miss Milroy.

MILLI. Everyone?

GODFREY. Yes. And he knows it.

(Pause.)

MILLI. He speaks well of you.

GODFREY. Really?

MILLI. He's fortunate to have a friend in you, Sir Thomas.

GODFREY. I would not assume such a station. I know my place, Miss Milroy.

MILLI. Pity.

GODFREY. Knowing one's place is what makes a civilisation great, Miss Milroy.

MILLI. For the few... Sir Thomas.

GODFREY. Ahh Yes... I take it you are one of those women who intends to vote?

MILLI. Yes, I'm one of those women.

GODFREY. Unfortunately, change comes with a price.

MILLI. I know.

GODFREY. Yes, I imagine you do, Miss Milroy.

(EDWARD returns laughing.)

EDWARD. Godfrey. I hope you did not bore Miss Milroy?

GODFREY. Sir. Miss Milroy, it was a pleasure.

MILLI. Likewise, Sir Thomas.

(GODFREY EXITS.)

EDWARD. Our hosts are terribly curious about you.

MILLI. Me?

EDWARD. They understand you are a princess of the House of Stewart.

MILLI. Why would they think that?

EDWARD. Something I might've said.

MILLI. What are you saying about me?

EDWARD. The first thing that pops into my head.

MILLI. You've been lying about me?

EDWARD. The truth would not last a minute in this place.

MILLI. They had better be good lies.

EDWARD. The most marvellous lies. I come from a long line of embellishers. *(Pause.)* I wish I were more like you, Miss Milroy, always telling the truth.

(MILLI smiles.)

EDWARD. What a mischievous look.

MILLI. Trying to look vacant.

EDWARD. Trying to evade.

MILLI. You have no idea what you're talking about.

EDWARD. Out with it.

MILLI. It's nothing...

EDWARD. Milli, you lied?

MILLI. No, not a lie.

EDWARD. But...

MILLI. When we first met...

EDWARD. Yes.

MILLI. When I first met you in the garden... I might have, hmmm... I might have...

EDWARD. You recognized me?!

MILLI. Not right away...

EDWARD. You recognized me!

MILLI. Not positively.

EDWARD. Milli.

MILLI. Just an inkling.

EDWARD. Two peas in a pod.

MILLI. I suppose this lowers your estimation of me.

EDWARD. Well, yes, though, not quite down to my level. Not yet.

QUEEN MILLI OF GALT

MILLI. I should have... What's that in your hand?

EDWARD. Nothing.

MILLI. *(She takes it from his hand.)* It's a spoon. You stole a spoon?

EDWARD. No. *(Pause.)* Yes, I suppose I did.

MILLI. You shouldn't steal.

EDWARD. Said the liar to the thief.

MILLI. Awfully plain. I would have thought you'd have better taste.

EDWARD. Used to be rather decorative. It's worn off.

MILLI. Worn off?

EDWARD. Had it since I was seven.

MILLI. Ahh. Started thievery at a young age?

EDWARD. Sort of a... good luck charm.

MILLI. The spoon?

EDWARD. You would not understand.

MILLI. Ah.

EDWARD. No, I take that back. You... you would. So... *(Pause.)* I was seven... having dinner. The family, the Prime Minister...

MILLI. Nicked it when no one was watching.

EDWARD. No, they were always watching. So... My father and the P.M. were having a heated discussion. Politics of some sort, and it degenerated into a screaming match as to what was the capital city of Ceylon. My father said that I would know and wagered one hundred pounds. I said "Colombo". An atlas was fetched and I was proved right. My father grabbed me, put me up on his knee and, using the spoon, dubbed me "Knight of Geography". Everyone else was dismissed, but I spent the rest of the evening on my father's knee while he discussed matters with the Prime Minister. *(Pause.)* I finally fell asleep there on his lap. I awoke in my bed still clutching the spoon. I felt loved for the first time.

MILLI. That's a wonderful story.

EDWARD. Years later, I realized... *(Pause.)* That night had nothing to do with me. Putting me on his knee, the knighting, the whole thing, was to "up his hand" with the P. M.... He used me to mock the Prime Minister. And that was it. I was going to throw it away. *(Pause.)* Then I thought... No! This is my proof of love. It was a lie. But I felt it. And that bastard wasn't going to take that away from me! Milli, feeling loved is better than being loved!

MILLI. Ah... David.

EDWARD. It's just a spoon.

MILLI. That's sad.·

EDWARD. I have an unbelievably privileged life. Nature requires some balance.

MILLI. Still...

EDWARD. Most men my age have experienced horrors of which I can scarcely even imagine. My feelings are an insult to their memory.

MILLI. No, they are not.

EDWARD. I invited you to this event because you loathe me. Please do not mar that with feelings of tenderness.

(Pause. They smile at an unseen guest.)

MILLI. Why do we play this game?

EDWARD. It is a society ball.

MILLI. No, I meant you and I.

EDWARD. So did I. You and I are a society ball. We act as if we didn't know what we both know.

MILLI. And that is?

EDWARD. Are you ready to stop playing the game?

MILLI. No.

(Both smile at an unseen guest.)

SCENE 15

(EDWARD'S RAIL CARRIAGE. Later that night. EDWARD is reading a Biography of himself. GODFREY enters quite distraught.)

GODFREY. Sir!

EDWARD. Ahh Godfrey, have you read this book?

GODFREY. Yes, Sir. Sir I need...

EDWARD. I don't even recognize me. Not a stitch of it is true.

GODFREY. It's the King, Sir.

EDWARD. You know, according to this, I'm an excellent marksman?

GODFREY. *(Overlapping.)* The... the... the King is...

EDWARD. The King is what?

GODFREY. Sir, the King is ill.

EDWARD. That my favourite author is Dostoevski?

GODFREY. *(Overlapping.)* Well he's... ah... sick... not well, Sir.

EDWARD. That I graduated top of my class at Osborne?

GODFREY. I will arrange for things.

EDWARD. What things?

GODFREY. Cancel the rest of the tour, and return home, Sir.

EDWARD. Why would I want to go home?

GODFREY. Because, the King is s-

EDWARD. I know, I know! The King is sick.

GODFREY. So, I'll arrange...

EDWARD. No.

GODFREY. Sir?

EDWARD. He has no use for me. I am not a doctor.

GODFREY. No. But... to be by his side at this time...

EDWARD. Has he summoned me?

GODFREY. Sir. *(Beat.)* If you would visit, it might lift his spirits...

EDWARD. No. The sight of me makes him feel ill when he is well. In a weakened state... A visit from me is likely to kill him.

GODFREY. But, Sir.

EDWARD. You want the King's death on your shoulders?

GODFREY. You are his son, Sir.

EDWARD. No. I am not his son! He is the King and I am the next in succession!

GODFREY. *(Pause.)* Well, Sir. I will... I will let you know when he recovers.

EDWARD. Don't bother. *(Pause.)* Do let me know if he dies, though.

GODFREY. Sir. *(Goes to EXIT.)*

EDWARD. It might comfort you to know that I am the... *(Reads from book.)* "shining emerald in my father's eye."

GODFREY. I, also, have a... *(Pause.)* with my father... also... Sir. *(Pause.)* Sir.

(GODFREY EXITS.)

SCENE 16

(MILLI'S PORCH. Two weeks later. MILLI is putting on one of MONA'S dresses.)

MILLI. *(O.S.)* I cannot go out of the house looking like this!

MONA. I think you look wonderful.

(MILLI comes out of the house.)

MILLI. I look like a harlot.

MONA. Thank you.

MILLI. No, no, on you this would look...

MONA. Like a harlot.

MILLI. No, it's just... I'm not used to seeing myself like this.

MONA. Just because you are a schoolteacher doesn't mean you have to look like one.

(She hands MILLI a hand mirror.)

MILLI. Wonderful. *(Pause.)* Mother will faint if she sees this.

MONA. So would most men.

MILLI. That's it! I can't wear this! What will Edward think?

MONA. What do you want him to think?

MILLI. What?

MONA. Are you falling for him?

MILLI. I feel nothing for that man.

MONA. You've seen him seven times in the last two weeks.

MILLI. Six.

MONA. Oh, I thought it was seven.

MILLI. I'm nothing more than a curiosity to him.There's nothing to... I like him, I'll give you that.

MONA. I've seen the way he looks at you. He's smitten.

MILLI. Intrigued by me, maybe. Taken... perhaps. But... *(Pause.)* But....

MONA. He loves you.

MILLI. He loves himself. *(Pause.)* No. Mona, I know what you want to believe but-

MONA. You just don't want to believe. He might not say it with his words, in fact...

MILLI. No, no, no, no! He, he loves the idea, maybe, the, the pursuit. Yes! Or, or, or the, the conquest! Yes, I'm just another conquest, one of many. This is what he was bred to do, to take on lands, to increase his empire! No. *(Beat.)* No flag is going in my soil. No. No. No.

MONA. So, are you going to wear the dress?

(MILLI looks hard at the dress frowning.)

MILLI. I don't know...

(MILLI'S frown breaks into a slight smile. MONA laughs.)

SCENE 17

(MILLI'S GARDEN. Late evening. EDWARD and Milli arrive on the porch. Milli is wearing the dress.)

MILLI. I had a good time.

EDWARD. You needn't end the evening with a lie.

MILLI. No, I... The speech you gave was... *(Pause.)* Not a dry eye in the place.

EDWARD. Yes, I was thinking...

MILLI. They were hanging on your every word.

EDWARD. God help me when I actually have something of worth to say.

MILLI. You do.

EDWARD. You give me too much credit.

MILLI. You give yourself too little.

EDWARD. Well...

MILLI. It was a good speech.

EDWARD. Not bad for an imbecile.

(MILLI laughs.)

EDWARD. I will miss that laugh, your candour... amongst other things. I'm off tomorrow. I suppose we shan't ever see...

QUEEN MILLI OF GALT

MILLI. Would you like to come in for tea? I might have some Lapsang...

(Several somewhat off-key voices start singing the hymn, "Bringing in the Sheaves.")

MILLI. Dear God.

EDWARD. What in heaven's name is that sound?

MILLI. Mother's Prayer Circle.

EDWARD. They're inside?

MILLI. Yes.

EDWARD. Oh hell.

MILLI. Oh yes.

EDWARD. I'd love to know what they're praying.

MILLI. Oh, no you wouldn't.

EDWARD. What?

MILLI. Nothing.

EDWARD. Now I simply have to know.

MILLI. They're praying...

EDWARD. Yes?

MILLI. They're praying that I'll be girded with the "breastplate of righteousness."

EDWARD. Horrid things, breastplates.

MILLI. You've...?

EDWARD. I own several.

MILLI. Yes of course.

EDWARD. Dreadfully uncomfortable. I'm forced to wear the blighted things twice a year. Oh, they look magnificent, but, bloody heavy. You can barely move. And they're absolutely frigid! Unless of course you're in the sun, well, then it's like wearing an oven! You get welts and blisters and... Milli, I can't even begin to imagine you in a breastplate. *(Beat.)* Well... Unless, it was in a... sort of a Joan of Arc... umm...

QUEEN MILLI OF GALT

(MILLI laughs.)

EDWARD. Duke of Cornwall.

MILLI. Sorry?

EDWARD. They just added Duke of Cornwall to my title, when I turned twenty-five.

MILLI. Ahhh. Duke of Cornwall, glad to make your acquaintance.

(MILLI puts out her hand and EDWARD kisses it. The Prayer Circle still singing away.)

EDWARD. Don't they know any other songs?

MILLI. Not all the way through.

EDWARD. Godfrey thinks you and I are sweethearts. Can you imagine that?

MILLI. No. *(Beat.)* Looking forward to going back home?

EDWARD. Dreading it.

MILLI. Oh.

EDWARD. It was terribly pleasing to escort a woman who didn't have any feelings...

MILLI. Actu...

EDWARD. ...for me. Heaven knows you have feelings... lots of them. Just... none for me.

MILLI. David?

EDWARD. Obviously we have some... *(Pause.)* Milli, if I asked what you really thought of... *(Nervously laughs.)* Milli, do you dislike me?

MILLI. There are a lot of things about your life I dislike.

EDWARD. That's not what I asked. I asked if you dislike me.

MILLI. *(Pause.)* I stopped disliking you some time ago.

EDWARD. Same here. I always look forward to our meetings.

MILLI. So do I. Don't get me wrong, I find you arrogant.

EDWARD. I find you prudish.

MILLI. I find you vain.
EDWARD. I find you...um... something.
MILLI. I find you...

(EDWARD kisses MILLI, who kisses back.)

MILLI. Pretentious and...

(MILLI pulls back slightly.)

EDWARD. Sorry, I didn't mean to... *(Kiss you.)*
MILLI. I didn't mean... *(To kiss back.)*
EDWARD. What do you...?
MILLI. It was a... a goodbye kiss.
EDWARD. Of course.
MILLI. And...
EDWARD. It means...
MILLI. Nothing...
EDWARD. Nothing.
MILLI. Friends kiss each other goodbye.
EDWARD. Yes, they do.
MILLI. We are just...

(Pause.)

EDWARD. Milli, is there something you want to say?

(Pause.)

MILLI. Yes.
EDWARD. What is it?
MILLI. Goodbye, David.

QUEEN MILLI OF GALT

(MILLI EXITS. EDWARD looks to where MILLI had gone.)

EDWARD. Goodbye Milli.

(SLOW FADE TO BLACK. The singing inside gets louder.)

SCENE 18

(MILLI'S PORCH. A short while later. MILLI is sitting on the steps. MRS. MILROY ENTERS and looks sheepishly at MILLI.)

MRS. MILROY. I'm sorry, dear. I didn't know what to do.

MILLI. I told you not to tell them!

MRS. MILROY. I don't want to see you hurt.

MILLI. We don't even like each other

MRS. MILROY. I asked God to guard your heart.

MILLI. I don't care for him that much.

MRS. MILROY. The women believe this was God's plan.

MILLI. Well, the prayer worked, he's gone. He's not coming back.

MRS. MILROY. But that wasn't the prayer, Dear. Mrs. Langhorn was praying... praying for you and the Prince of Wales. She had a vision of Jonah. Milli, Jonah! Jonah was swallowed by a whale. "The Prince-of-Wales"? Hmmm? I just... I thought you should know.

MILLI. Yes, now I know.

MRS. MILROY. So, so you understand what it means?

MILLI. Yes. You prayed that I wouldn't be swallowed by the whale.

MRS. MILROY. No, we prayed that you would be swallowed.

MILLI. You...?

MRS. MILROY. Milli, God used the whale to take Jonah where he didn't want to go, but where he was meant to be. Milli, God used the whale. God can use the Prince.

(Pause.)

MILLI. But he's not coming back.

SCENE 19

(EDWARD'S RAIL CARRIAGE. The next morning. The train on its way to New York. GODFREY ENTERS with a paper.)

GODFREY. Your paper, Sir.
EDWARD. No, thanks.
GODFREY. London Times, Sir. Just six days old.
EDWARD. Not this morning.
GODFREY. You and Miss Milroy said a proper goodbye, Sir?
EDWARD. We said goodbye.
GODFREY. The tour went well.
EDWARD. Yes.
GODFREY. Now if you can win over the Yanks.
EDWARD. Hmmm.
GODFREY. Hard, aren't they, Sir?
EDWARD. Are they?
GODFREY. Goodbyes, Sir. Always hard.
EDWARD. Yes. Yes, they are.
GODFREY. Always hard. She was a good woman.
EDWARD. That she is.
GODFREY. *(Pause.)* The tour went well, Sir.

EDWARD. A first rate stunt.

GODFREY. What? Ah yes... The Canadians seemed to really take to you, Sir.

EDWARD. They did.

GODFREY. Not hard to see why.

EDWARD. Yes, everyone loves the Prince of Wales.

GODFREY. Ending it was the right thing.

EDWARD. There was nothing to end.

GODFREY. Yet hard nonetheless.

EDWARD. Yes.

GODFREY. I'm saying this in... as a... in friendship, Sir.

EDWARD. Yes.

GODFREY. I am not speaking out of turn?

EDWARD. No. You're right; we *(Milli and I.)* are... friends.

GODFREY. Friends. Yes, friends. Yes, and friends... they, they... talk, they talk about things that are somewhat personal, and are ahh... personal.

EDWARD. We are... good friends.

GODFREY. And I think of you, Sir, if I may be so bold, as a... as a good friend too.

EDWARD. What? Ah, yes, right, good...

GODFREY. I've been thinking for some time now, that... well... Sir. I know Lord Hamilton and the Admiral call you Eddie and Lord Mountbatten call you David, as did Miss Milroy. I would not dream of calling you Eddie and certainly not David. But, as a friend, I would be honoured to be able to call you... Edward. Not in front of others, but when we are alone, as we often are, I would like to call you Edward, Sir, if that would be to your liking, if you have no objections.

EDWARD. No, I have no objections.

GODFREY. This has made me...

EDWARD. *(Laughing.)* It is dead confusing... trying to remember what to call me. I'm confused myself.

GODFREY. Yes. Yes, I'll make a conc-

QUEEN MILLI OF GALT

EDWARD. Yes, let's just keep it simple, hmmm? My life is getting so complicated. Let's just keep things the way they are.

GODFREY. *(Pause.)* Um... yes, that would be... simpler...

(EDWARD starts reading his paper.)

GODFREY. *(Pause.)* It's good to keep things simple. *(Pause.)* I have your New York speech to write. *(Godfrey goes to exit, stops, turns around.)* Good day, Sir.

(Godfrey EXITS. EDWARD puts down paper.)

EDWARD. Good day, Godfrey.

SCENE 20

(MILLI'S GARDEN. Two weeks later. MILLI is on her knees with a trowel. EDWARD ENTERS covered in mud, wearing khaki overcoat, driving gloves and goggles, and a cap. EDWARD watches MILLI gardening for a while before he speaks.)

EDWARD. What a beautiful sugar maple.

MILLI. *(Pause.)* Is it you?

EDWARD. Yes, Milli. I wanted to surprise you, which I seem to have done.

MILLI. No, I thought you were... *(Jonathan.)* I didn't know it was you.

EDWARD. It's me. Back from the dead... Well, back from Buffalo.

MILLI. I thought you were sailing today.

EDWARD. The ship has been delayed, so we're stuck in Buffalo for a week. And, oddly enough, we couldn't find any

MILLI. Any what?

EDWARD. Buffalos, there are no buffalos in Buffalo. Plenty of Buffalonians mind you. Anyway... I had some time on my hands and not much to do, so I bought three roadsters! Decided to have a race.

MILLI. From Buffalo... that's a whole day's journey!

EDWARD. Seven hours. Mine has quite a little kick in her.

MILLI. You're absolutely covered in mud.

EDWARD. Yes, got stuck a ditch. But I managed to make my way out of the muck. And, I believe, I might have won the race. *(Pause.)* I have a gift for you.

(EDWARD hands MILLI a burlap pouch. She pulls out something that looks like a stick with thick gnarly roots.)

EDWARD. Yes I know. It's the ugliest gift any man has given any woman.

MILLI. It's a rootstock.

EDWARD. The Royal Botanical Society has named a new rose after me. I could describe its beauty, but, it's best that you see for yourself. I promise... just a little mud, a smidgen of water, and the barest scrap of love will turn my vile little gift into a bouquet of roses.

MILLI. It's perfect. Thank you.

(MILLI stands and is not too sure what to do; hug or shake hands.)

MILLI. We should plant it.

EDWARD. Now you mean? Yes, why not. You know how much I love gardening... the idea.

(MILLI laughs.)

EDWARD. So, what first? I suppose we...

QUEEN MILLI OF GALT

MILLI. Dig a hole.

EDWARD. Right, dig a hole. Given enough time, I would have figured that part out.

MILLI. Use the trowel

EDWARD. Right. I suppose I need gloves... Ahhh *(Pulls out his riding gloves.)* Italian riding gloves should do the trick.

MILLI. Loosen up the soil and add compost.

(EDWARD starts digging a hole.)

EDWARD. *(Looks at root stock.)* Looks dead.

MILLI. It's dormant.

EDWARD. Yes, of course.

EDWARD. I have the most dreadful news. *(Pause.)* I believe I just might love you! Yes I know, it's terribly sad, and simply horrid and, and, worse yet... True. I suppose this is deep enough? I'm sorry Milli, but... *(Pause.)* This silly little boy loves you. Godfrey would say... "The Prince has expressed his love, you must reciprocate." But I would say "Take your time, Miss Milroy."

(EDWARD picks up root stock.)

EDWARD. *(To root stock.)* I know you're dormant but... do what you can for your namesake, hmm?

(EDWARD puts root stock in the hole and starts to fill hole up.)

EDWARD. You have not told me you love me, but I feel you love me. Milli, it is better to feel love then to have it said. That being said, I... *(Pause.)*

(MILLI starts to cry.)

MILLI. I was... I was at Orr Lake last week... *(Pause.)* There was only one swan.

(MILLI slowly makes her way back to EDWARD sobbing.)

MILLI.. But... you're here. You are here.

(They kiss.)

MILLI. You came back.

(A single leaf falls.)

SCENE 21

(ORR LAKE. One week later. There is the sound of water lapping. EDWARD and MILLI are having a picnic. EDWARD is fishing.)

MILLI. No, no, no. Again.
EDWARD. All right, listen... Splendid.
MILLI. Splendid.
EDWARD. Try it again.
MILLI. Splendid.

(EDWARD laughs.)

MILLI. What? What did I say?
EDWARD. You said "splandid".
MILLI. I said splendid. Not "splandid".
EDWARD. Well, it sounded like "splandid" to me. Hmmm. Try...

try... wonderful.
    MILLI. Wonderful.
    EDWARD. Oh no, you'll never do.
    MILLI. That's it! We're mismatched.
    EDWARD. Oh no... that look, I believe I'm just about to get a kiss.

(MILLI bites EDWARD softly on the ear.)

    EDWARD. What was that? A bite?
    MILLI. A nibble.

(There is the sound of a swan calling in the distance.)

    MILLI. Hear that? That was her.
    EDWARD. Where is she?
    MILLI. Around the bend there. She'll make her way here later...
Myrtle's used to me.
    EDWARD. She sounds lonely.
    MILLI. Yes.
    EDWARD. Well, she'll find a mate soon enough.
    MILLI. Probably not.
    EDWARD. Oh?
    MILLI. They're quite rare. They were lucky to find each other.
    EDWARD. Hmmm. *(Pause.)* It's been a wonderful week.
    MILLI. *(Milli caresses EDWARD'S hands.)* Your hands are callused.
Don't tell me you've been working?
    EDWARD. Pump handling.
    MILLI. Hmmm?
    EDWARD. Shaking hands.
    MILLI. Really?
    EDWARD. Sometimes it can actually accomplish something.
(Pause.) I've started to rather enjoy being the Prince of Wales. I actually
had a sincere feeling. It's perfectly loathsome. I've become... what's that

word... umm... Good! I've become good. It's horrid. And I have you to blame for that. Case in point, last week I was giving out medals... *(ED-WARD kisses Milli's neck.)* hmmm?

MILLI. Lavender.

EDWARD. Ahhh... Lavender... Mmmm... You smell like a French girl. *(Pause.)* That came out odd.

MILLI. You were giving out medals?

EDWARD. Yes, and well, yes, I got to the end of the line and they were one medal short. So I- without thinking- took off one of mine and pinned it on the soldier. I said to him, "you are more deserving of it than I". It seems, that one small act was the breach of a dozen protocols. The King was livid! His telegram was to the point, "You will be David the rest of your life"

MILLI. What's that supposed to mean?

EDWARD. He calls me David because I'm not worthy of the Edward name.

MILLI. You're more than worthy...

EDWARD. Not regal enough.

MILLI. David is quite a wonderful name.

EDWARD. Yes, I could be David the rest of my life...

MILLI. King David.

EDWARD. Yes, your mother's Prayer Circle would love that... King David. Yes, King David and Queen Milli.

MILLI. David?

EDWARD. Milli. Will you be my wife?

MILLI. Wife?

EDWARD. Yes, I was going to say, "Will you be my Princess". I get to say rot like that.

MILLI. Your wife?

EDWARD. I actually wrote something, you know a, "I love you... foundations of the earth... time..."

MILLI. You're... serious?

EDWARD. Yes, I actually wrote something down. It was vaguely

QUEEN MILLI OF GALT

poetic, intimate...

MILLI. David...

EDWARD. Exactly, pretentious. I thought, no, "Just keep it simple". So. What say you?

(MILLI smiles unable to speak.)

EDWARD. I have this habit of sucking the words right out of you. *(Pause.)* Suggestion: "Oh yes, David. Oh David, this is the happiest day of my life, David". Or, "David I am so very, very, very...

MILLI. Shut up. *(Gives EDWARD a kiss.)* Yes.

EDWARD. "Shut up. Yes" is fine. Not quite "Oh, David I'm the happiest woman in the world", but... *(Beat.)* Milli, I will love you, always.

MILLI. And I you.

(EDWARD pulls in MILLI close.)

EDWARD. I'm expecting the King's response today.

MILLI. You asked his permission?

EDWARD. No, I told him my decision.

(LIGHTS FADE a swan calls in the distance.)

SCENE 22

(MILLI'S GARDEN. A few hours later. GODFREY is pacing. MRS. MILROY and MONA are sitting.)

MRS. MILROY. Would you like some more tea, Sir Thomas?

QUEEN MILLI OF GALT

GODFREY. No thank you, Mrs. Milroy.

MRS. MILROY. It's just a matter of boiling a "spot" of water.

GODFREY. I'm fine... Thank you.

MRS. MILROY. We have a gas stove.

GODFREY. It's getting dark.

MONA. I think they'll be fine.

GODFREY. I should go and search again.

MONA. They've only been gone for a few hours.

GODFREY. The train in Buffalo is waiting.

MONA. I thought it was his train.

GODFREY. What? Yes, yes, of course, but we have a schedule to maintain.

MONA. Of course.

GODFREY. Miss Singleton, how did he seem to you?

MONA. Seem?

GODFREY. His mood!

MRS. MILROY. He seemed happy.

MONA. ... "Down right chipper".

GODFREY. Really?

MONA. Like a schoolboy on the first day of summer.

GODFREY. Hmmm...

MONA. As far as I could tell... Sir Thomas

MRS. MILROY. Don't worry, they should be back soon.

GODFREY. I am not worried.

MONA. Funny, you look worried.

GODFREY. No, we just have a...

MONA. -schedule *(Shed-ule.)* to maintain?

MRS. MILROY. They grow up so fast...

(GODFREY paces. MRS. MILROY and MONA watch.)

MRS. MILROY. I find tea soothes the nerves.

MONA. Or Scotch.

QUEEN MILLI OF GALT

(MILLI and EDWARD enter laughing.)

EDWARD. Mrs. Milroy, Mona, sorry we seem to have been delayed... Godfrey?

GODFREY. Sir. I had no... I didn't know your whereabouts and I was concerned about your... schedule.

EDWARD. Sir Thomas worries about me too much.

GODFREY. Well then, Sir. We need to go.

EDWARD. Later.

GODFREY. Sir if you please-

EDWARD. Mona. I've put the jazz steps you taught me to great use. For what it's worth, you are my second favourite dance partner in the country.

MONA. Thank you, Your Highness.

EDWARD. Oh, no, David. Here I am David.

MONA. Thank you, David.

EDWARD. Mrs Milroy, is it possible that you are looking younger every day? Mrs Milroy, this is for you.

(EDWARD hands MRS. MILROY a small box.)

MRS. MILROY. Oh, David, you shouldn't have.

(MRS. MILROY takes box and quickly opens it and pulls out a necklace.)

MRS. MILROY. These are... These are... Oh my... Crown Jewels?

EDWARD. A Crown's jewel, not the Crown Jewels.

MONA. They're beautiful Mrs. Milroy.

MRS. MILROY. Oh, but they're, they're real?

EDWARD. We've never thought to have them authenticated.

MRS. MILROY. I shall never wear them. They are much too valuable.

EDWARD. Think of them as too valuable not to wear.

MRS. MILROY. I shall wear them. Ooh yes. Thank you, *(Beat.)* David. This is such a wonderful gift.

EDWARD. Oh, Mrs. Milroy, I fear you have misunderstood. This is not a gift.

MRS. MILROY. Oh I... I...

EDWARD. No, these are a bribe, Mrs. Milroy.

MRS. MILROY. A bribe?

EDWARD. I desire something much more valuable in return. What I want from you is Milli's hand.

MONA. Oh Milli!

EDWARD. The rest of her as well, but... you know...

MRS. MILROY. Ooh, ooh... ooh... ooh...

EDWARD. I'll take that as a yes.

MONA. This is so romantic.

GODFREY. *(To EDWARD.)* What are you doing?

EDWARD. *(To GODFREY.)* Making a decision.

MONA. Mrs. Milroy, Milli's going to be a Princess.

MRS. MILROY. Ooh... ooh...

EDWARD. Are you all right Mrs. Milroy?

MRS. MILROY. A Princess? Then a, a Qu... A Queen... Oh my.

GODFREY. *(Quietly.)* Sir. Please, Sir.

MRS. MILROY. I'll be the Queen Mother! Oh... Oh...

EDWARD. *(Quietly.)* not here.

MONA. You'll make a wonderful Queen Mother.

MRS. MILROY. Mona's been helping me with my diction haven't you? "The yellow bird is quite pleasant to view..."

GODFREY. *(Quietly.)* You have a telegram.

MRS. MILROY. "We will be entwined with wondrous words of wit".

EDWARD. *(Quietly.)* Not now.

MRS. MILROY. "The sly serpent speaks and sovereigns shall sink".

MONA. That's very good, Mrs. Milroy.

GODFREY. FROM THE KING! SIR.

EDWARD. Ahhh. It seems the King misses me already.

MRS. MILROY. A telegram from the King?

EDWARD. Yes... the King.

MRS. MILROY. Oh... Do read it.

EDWARD. Maybe later.

MRS. MILROY. The Prayer Circle has been interceding for the King for the last month.

EDWARD. Well, maybe, maybe God has softened the King's heart. Maybe.

MRS. MILROY. Maybe God is testing you!

GODFREY. Perhaps we shall have that tea now.

MONA. Mrs. Milroy I'll help you.

MRS MILROY. Oh yes! English Breakfast? Is it all right to serve English Breakfast in the afternoon? I'll just boil a "spot" of water...

(MONA and MRS. MILROY EXIT.)

GODFREY. Sir. The telegram was encoded.

EDWARD. We shall not let Him infect this moment. Just by the look on Godfrey's face I know what it contains. What did he call me this time? What? "A useless sod"? Is that right, Godfrey?

GODFREY. Sir.

EDWARD. All right.

(GODFREY hands EDWARD the telegram.)

EDWARD reads. Silence.

MILLI. What is it David? *(Pause.)* David?

(Pause.)

GODFREY. Miss Milroy. *(Pause.)* The King has declined permission.

(Pause.)

GODFREY. His Royal Highness cannot take you as his wife.

MILLI. David?

GODFREY. The Prince of Wales has a destiny, Miss Milroy. *(Pause.)* The choice has been taken from his hands.

MILLI. You are free to do whatever you want.

GODFREY. If The Prince defies The King, he will be stripped of everything.

MILLI. Not everything.

GODFREY. Do you understand Miss Milroy? All titles! Edward will cease to be the Prince of Wales!

EDWARD. God Damn the King.

GODFREY. It was inevitable, Sir.

EDWARD. Inevitable? *(Pause.)* I know what to do. I know... Milli, we can marry in secret.

MILLI. But David...

EDWARD. We don't have to tell the King. We don't have to tell anyone. I know a priest. You can be my wife... and what the King does not know...

GODFREY. He will find out! He has ears...

EDWARD. *(Overlapping.)* No, he will not!

GODFREY. EVERYWHERE! *(Long pause.)* Sir.

(GODFREY EXITS.)

EDWARD. Godfrey? *(Pause.)* No one has to know Milli.

MILLI. We'll be forced to live a lie.

EDWARD. My whole life is a lie. It's the only way.

MILLI. David, they'll find out.

EDWARD. I know. I... know. He's gone too far. I can... *(Pause.)* I can give it all up! Everything Milli. Everything! The titles, the throne, my family! I will give it all up for you.

MILLI. David, you cannot do this.

EDWARD. This is one thing I can do!

MILLI. You can't give everything up for me.

EDWARD. If you love me you will do the right thing.

MILLI. This is the right thing.

EDWARD. You love me. We can do this.

MILLI. I'm sorry.

EDWARD. Milli Please.

MILLI. No.

EDWARD. If you cannot marry me, then right here I'll make a vow. I, David, take you, Milli to be my wife! To love you forever.

MILLI. No.

EDWARD. Milli... Milli, my vows are real. Nothing can change that

MILLI. Just leave! Don't... Don't come back! Just...

EDWARD. You love me, you felt it.

MILLI. It only felt like love!

(Long pause.)

EDWARD. It is love.

MILLI. *(Whispers.)* David... please go... please...

EDWARD. In my heart you are my wife, Milli, in my heart.

MILLI. Goodbye.

EDWARD. I will love you always.

MILLI. Goodbye...Your Highness.

(EDWARD stands frozen, lost. He slowly EXITS. EDWARD is gone. MILLI is weeping. MILLI transforms into OLD MILLI. Light shift.)

QUEEN MILLI OF GALT

SCENE 23

(MILLI'S GARDEN 1919 turns to 1972. OLD MILLI and JOURNALIST.)

OLD MILLI. His train left. And once more there was an ocean between us. And once more a cold angry girl... I never saw him again. But, he never quite... left *(me.)* He continued to write for... for years. Faithfully. I didn't open them... Couldn't. *(Pause.)* The letters stopped in 1930... April... *(Pause.)* April. *(JOURNALIST comes out of the shadows.)*

JOURNALIST. Wallis Simpson...? That's when he met Wallis Simpson. *(Pause.)* You... you look like her.

OLD MILLI. No... *(Pause.)* She looked like me. *(Long pause.)* A few months ago, I read the news... *(Pause.)* I was surprised... *(Pause.)* Fifty years... Fifty... *(Pause.)* The papers said he died quietly... in his sleep. *(Pause.)* There was a picture of him *(Beat.)* working in his garden. *(Pause.)* I had his letters, hundreds of them... Unopened. Unread. *(Pause.)* I made a bon-fire, clearing out the past. One letter at a time, into the fire... Gone. I wondered what words they contained *(Pause. She starts crying softly.)* What thoughts... what feelings... *(Pause.)* I continued to feed the fire. His words. Ashes. *(Pause.)* And then... he was gone. But... Last week... *(Slowly.)* One final word came. A small parcel from his estate. *(Pause.)* His spoon.

(MILLI holds up EDWARD'S teaspoon.)

OLD MILLI. And so the tombstone... *(Pause.)* I'm tired, it's late, *(Pause.)* Goodbye.

(The JOURNALIST goes to exit, he stops, turns around, he is about to ask another question, but sees Old Milli is lost in thought. He smiles and EXITS.)

QUEEN MILLI OF GALT

(MILLI holds up EDWARD'S spoon. She slowly starts to dance... to dream...)

OLD MILLI. I missed you. *(Pause.)* I feel... Loved.

(A blizzard of leaves fall. Slow fade to black.)

THE END

QUEEN MILLI OF GALT

Costumes Plot

THE JOURNALIST
Casual and somewhat scruffy 70's Jacket and slacks (Scenes 1 & 23)

OLD MILLI
A shawl over Young Milli's clothes. (Scenes 1 & 23)

MILLI
Gardening clothes. A simple blue dress, gardening gloves. She wears rubber boots and Jonathan's old brown sweater except in scenes 21 & 22 where she wears walking shoes. (Scenes 2, 4, 6, 7, 20, 21, 22)

The lilac colored dress. A collar is added for the classroom scene. (Scenes 9, 10, 12)

The Ball gown. Grand and elegant. (Scenes 13 & 14)

Mona's dress. An outrageous drop dead gorgeous dress in a flapper style. (Scenes 16, 17, 18)

EDWARD
A stylish well fitting suit. Edward was known for being a fashion horse (See period photos) (Scenes 3, 5, 7, 8, 9)

Edwards casual suit with a flamboyant shirt and tie (Scenes 11, 12)

Tuxedo and tails with white tie. (Scenes 13, 14, 17)

Silk robe and slippers (Scene 15, 19)

Khaki overcoat, driving gloves and goggles, and a cap. (Worn over casual suit) (Scene 20)

Edwards casual suit with an earth-tone shirt and flowery tie. (21,22)

MRS. MILROY
Her dress is about 20 years old; dark colored, stiff

Victorian style with a small hat. In scene 9 she wears a larger somewhat ridiculous hat with feathers. (Scenes 2, 9, 18, 22)

QUEEN MILLI OF GALT

MONA
Outrageous colorful and sexy. Flapper style (Scene 3)
Courtesan Costume: Feathers and veils. (Scene 9)
Mona Casual: slightly less outrageous (Scenes 16, 22)

GODFREY
Simple dark suit. (Scenes 3, 5, 8, 9, 11, 15, 19, 22)
Tuxedo with white tie and tails (Scenes 13, 14)

QUEEN MILLI OF GALT

Prop List

1. Notebook and pencil
2. Tea service
3. Gardening tools and trowel
4. Basket of bulbs
5. Root stock
6. Godfrey's schedule book
7. Edward's spoon.
8. Copy of The Woman of Destiny Lane (The play is fictional)
9. Mona's dance cards
10. 2 telegrams
11. 3 Handwritten notes and one small photo
12. A pointer
13. Loose change
14. Godfrey's watch
15. Edward's hard covered pocket sized Biography
16. Hand mirror
17. London Times
18. Burlap pouch with a rose root stock
19. Picnic basket
20. Fishing rod
21. Small box with a necklace

OTHER TITLES AVAILABLE FROM SAMUEL FRENCH

MURDER AMONG FRIENDS
Bob Barry

Comedy Thriller / 4m, 2f / Interior

Take an aging, exceedingly vain actor; his very rich wife; a double dealing, double loving agent, plunk them down in an elegant New York duplex and add dialogue crackling with wit and laughs, and you have the basic elements for an evening of pure, sophisticated entertainment. Angela, the wife and Ted, the agent, are lovers and plan to murder Palmer, the actor, during a contrived robbery on New Year's Eve. But actor and agent are also lovers and have an identical plan to do in the wife. A murder occurs, but not one of the planned ones.

"Clever, amusing, and very surprising."
– *New York Times*

"A slick, sophisticated show that is modern and very funny."
– WABC TV